CATHY

CLOVER SPRINGS MAIL ORDER BRIDES 11

RACHEL WESSON

LONDONGATE PUBLISHING

Created with Vellum

CHAPTER 1

NEW YORK, MARCH 1888

"Miss, please wake up. Come on, Miss Catherine. We don't have much time"

"Leave me be. I want to sleep." Catherine pulled the covers back over her head.

"Miss, get out of that bed at once. You owe it to your parents."

Catherine sat up straight. "My parents are dead. Don't you dare talk about them."

"Miss Catherine, you will be dead soon, too, if you stay here. Now, come on. It's all planned, remember. Toby is downstairs waiting with the carriage. I have your bag."

"Where's my medicine?"

"You had it already."

Catherine tried to focus on the servant girl. She couldn't remember her name. Was it Jane? Yes, it was. She couldn't remember most things, but she knew she hadn't had anything this morning. Before she could protest, Jane was urging her to hurry up.

"Miss Catherine, you are putting us all in danger. Please. For our sake, move now. We have to get out of here before he comes back."

Catherine got up and allowed the servant to dress her. She wasn't sure where she was going, but her instinct was to do as Jane told her. Jane had been with her mother for years. She had started in the house at age twelve and worked her way up from kitchen helper. She'd been her mother's personal maid. Mama. She was dead. Papa, too.

"Jane, are you coming with me?"

"No, Miss, I can't. I have to stay here. I got my family to think of. But you will be fine. Your sister will look after you."

"My sister? I don't have any sisters."

"Yes, Miss, you do. Remember? She lives in Clover Springs. Now, take your bag and your train ticket. Don't lose that purse I gave you. It has your money in it. Toby sold that jewelry you gave me. He didn't get much for it but it's better than nothing. He couldn't risk Master Archibald finding out about the sale."

With a last look at her home, Catherine left. Toby gave her a hand up in to the carriage. He had a kind face. He had bought her ticket and put her on the train to Denver. She had to change there to get the train to Clover Springs.

She moaned as she lifted her head. The feeling of tiredness was worse than ever. She needed a couple of drops of her medicine. She had hidden it in the bag despite what Jane had said. The doctor had given it to her to help dull the pain of losing her parents.

What she doing on the train? Oh, yes. She was going to see her sister. In Clover Springs, Colorado. She asked the ticket man to wake her when they got there. He seemed nice. Her eyes closed and soon she was in a restless world of darkness once more.

CHAPTER 2

NOELLE, COLORADO MARCH 1888

Abe O'Malley took a final look at the graves before turning his back and getting on his horse. He rode away without a backwards glance. He had done what he promised. Stayed and looked after Sally's family until they were all gone. It was time to leave Noelle and all the memories, good and bad behind him.

He just had one more stop to make and then he would go and never come back. He rode out to the house near the mine. It looked better than it had in years. Cara and Ma worked hard keeping the gardens and the house tidy. As he pulled up, the door opened and his little sister came running out, braids flying behind her.

"Abe, Ma said you wouldn't call but I knew you would. You couldn't leave without saying goodbye."

For all her confident words, he caught the uncertainty in her eyes.

"Course I wouldn't go without saying goodbye to my favorite girl in the whole world."

"Judes's here. He wanted to eat Ma's apple pie but she said she wasn't cutting it until you got here."

He smiled, thinking of how his brother would react to that. He still couldn't believe Jude was an officer of the law. The youngster had got into more scraps than most boys his age but he had turned out real smart with a good heart. He was the youngest deputy sheriff for miles around, but then most didn't want a job in Leadville with all the trouble.

Like Abe, he had a soft spot for women who needed protection. Many a fellow found themselves inside a cell for the night, protesting it wasn't against the law to hit their missus. It wasn't, either, but that never bothered Jude any. If he caught wind of a wife beater, that man would spend time in the cells for something or other.

Cara took his horse and led her off to the barn, where she would give her some oats and fresh water. His little sister was mad about animals. At times, his ma got frustrated with her as she refused to kill a chicken or be present when they butchered a pig. *Some wife she'll make* was his ma's favorite saying but Abe knew, as they all did, Cara held a special place in his ma's heart. Her birth had marked a turn-around in ma's fortunes, not least because that was the same night his pa died.

He didn't want to think of Fergus O'Malley now. He forced a smile on his face and walked up to the door. Ma hadn't come outside to greet him. That was her way of telling him she didn't agree with his plans. But she wouldn't beg him not to go. Ellen O'Malley never asked for anything for herself.

He put the bag of foodstuffs and other things he had purchased from the store in town beside the door. He might be leaving but he had made sure his ma and Cara would be fine for the next few months.

"Evening, Jude," he remarked to his brother.

"About time you got here. Can we have pie now, Ma?" Jude raised his coffee cup. "The prodigal son is here."

He didn't take offense to Jude's teasing. He knew there was no malice in it. They got on well despite the gap in age.

"Sit down and eat your meal. It's a bit crispy around the edges."

"Thanks, Ma. It smells great."

He wasn't hungry, but that didn't matter. He had to eat the meal. He ate quickly so Jude could have his slice of pie.

"That was lovely, Ma. Sit down, will you? Jude can get you a cup of coffee."

"Why can't you do it? I've been working hard all week," Jude replied, then immediately turned red. "Sorry, Brother. I didn't think. I just opened my mouth and let the words rush out."

"No matter," he said quickly, hoping to change the subject. "Ma, you got credit at the store to keep you going for a while. When I am sorted, I will send some money back. Jude and the boys will also chip in."

"That will be the day. Charlie is never out of the boozer."

"Cara, don't speak about your brother like that. He will do what he can," Ma reprimanded his sister.

He didn't comment on his younger brother who was turning out to the image of Fergus. He never called that man Pa. What Cara said was true, but if Ma wanted to ignore the fact one of her sons was drinking himself into the grave, who was he to stop her? He was fed up being responsible for the O'Malley tribe. He had done his bit. Mary, his sister, was happily married, the boys were in the main, all working. Jude would keep an eye on Ma and Cara.

"I best get going, Ma."

"Stay tonight and set out early in the morning. It will be safer."

That was probably true, but he didn't want to prolong the agony of leaving. He had already waited a year from when he first lost Sally. His ma had insisted with time, he would find it easier to stay in Noelle, but that wasn't the case. His ma and Cara would cry and he'd had enough of tears.

"Where are you heading first, Abe?"

"Clover Springs. I want to ask Cookie and Mick to come visit Doc. He isn't the same. The last year has taken its toll. His missus, Cara, is worried."

"I love Aunt Cara. She is really good to me. I am named after her."

"Yes, you are sweetheart and a nicer lady you'd struggle to meet. Say hello to Mick and Cookie for us, son."

"I will, Ma."

"I'll ride a bit of the way with you, Abe."

He nodded in response to Jude before pulling his ma into a hug. "Take care of yourself, Ma. I got to do this."

"I know you think you do, son, but you can't run away from your head."

She might be right, but he could try. He gave Cara

a hug, too. She was already crying. "Diamond is ready for you. I gave her extra oats."

With a lump in his throat he mounted his horse, and together he and Jude rode out. Neither looked back.

CHAPTER 3

CLOVER SPRINGS, APRIL 1888

"Doc Erin, about time you came back," Wilma cried as she pulled Erin in a big hug. "I missed you and Alicia and the children something dreadful."

"What about me and Aaron?"

"You be quiet, Mick Quinn. Don't you know I done missed you two handsome men as well," Wilma said before screaming as Mick lifted her up and swung her around. "You put me down. Right now, you hear."

"Let her go. Stop hurting her." Before Mick could do anything, two little girls—one white, one black—attacked him, kicking at his ankles. One bit his arm, leaving wet bite marks on his jacket. "What the heck?"

"Amy, Suzy, stop that this instant. Mick be a friend of your Grammy."

Erin and Mick stared at Wilma first before looking at the young girls and then back at her. She wrapped her arms around the little ones' shoulders.

"Mick, Erin, I would like you to meet my granddaughters. They be a bit protective of me. They is finding it difficult settling in here in Clover Springs."

"We don't like it here. We want to go home."

Erin watched as Mick bent down to the girls' level. Holding out his hand to shake theirs, he said, "Well, now, I don't like to hear that. I love Clover Springs and want everyone else to love it, too. Have we not been nice to you?"

Amy shook her head, her copper colored braids almost hitting Mick in the face. Suzy just stared at him.

"How you hurt your leg? You walk funny."

"Suzy, that's not nice." Wilma reprimanded her granddaughter.

"Aw, Wilma, don't chide her. She is only stating the obvious." Mick winked at Suzy who amazingly smiled back at him. Wilma seemed pleased they were back. The children must be giving her problems. Erin wanted to ask her friend how her health was but it wasn't appropriate in front of the children.

"I was in a fight and hurt it real bad. But a good doctor helped me fix it." Mick was still bent down at the children's level. She knew he would find that painful.

"Is she your doctor? Grammy Wilma called her Doc."

Erin hid a smile at the clever child.

"Aren't you a clever little lady? Do you mind if I sit down for a while as my knee hurts trying to sit like this." Suzy nodded solemnly, even moving slightly so he could sit on the chair nearest to where she was standing.

"No, Doc Erin is my wife. Now, why don't you tell me why you don't like Clover Springs? Maybe I can help fix it so you do."

"Bertram Shaw."

Erin saw Wilma bite her lip as the two girls spoke at the same time. Mick glanced at her and she nodded. "Go on, girls, tell Mick what's been happening. He doesn't like Master Shaw much either."

"He is being really mean. He says Grammy can't be my Grammy cause I is white. And he says Suzy can't be my twin sister. But she is. We was born at the same time to the same mama. That makes us twins."

"It sure does. So you know Bertram is talking rot. Why are you listening to him?"

Erin tried not to laugh at the look of consternation

on the twins' faces. They obviously hadn't seen it that way before.

"But he shouldn't say it. We tried to slap his mouth but we got into trouble."

"Miss Templeton didn't like that, huh?" Mick asked.

"She ain't our teacher. Our teacher is Mrs. Barrett. She's nice, but she said we can't hit Bertram or anyone else."

"Mrs. Barrett? Seems like we missed a lot when we were away, Wilma."

"You sure did, Doc Erin. We had us a fine wedding. Gary, he be busy building a house next to the school for him, Eleanor, Rosa, and John."

"They got married and adopted Rosa and John as well? I must go over and see if I can help with the house," Mick said.

"Gary would welcome that, Mick."

"Would you two girls like to come with me? Maybe you can tell me more about what you don't like about Clover Springs and we will find a way of fixing it."

Wilma nodded as the twins looked at her for permission. "You be good, girls. Mick doesn't like badly-behaved young'uns."

"We will, Grammy. We always are."

"They seem like nice girls, Wilma."

"Despite their innocent little faces, they aren't

always." She sighed. "When the twins want to be good, they are no problem to anyone. The problem is they seem to enjoy making trouble. Not just for themselves but for other people."

"They are just settling in to their new environment. It will take a while." Erin sought to reassure her friend.

"Wilma, make sure you keep me some of those oatmeal cookies. I built up an appetite in New York for your fine cooking."

Erin smiled as Mick left, a girl on either side holding his hands. "Wilma, sit down and stop fussing. I want to hear all your news," Erin said.

CHAPTER 4

The door opened and in walked Mrs. Grey, closely followed by Father Molloy.

"Knew it wouldn't take long for you to smell the cookies." Wilma teased Father Molloy as he greeted Erin like a long-lost daughter. Mrs. Grey also gave Erin a hug before taking a seat.

"Saw Mick walking down the street with the girls. They look happier today," Mrs. Grey said.

"They seem like lovely girls, Wilma. How did you find them?"

"It's a long story, Erin."

"Don't forget to tell her about your upcoming wedding," Mrs. Grey added.

"Lorena Grey, you never know when to keep quiet, do ya?" Wilma exclaimed as Erin coughed and spluttered, the coffee she had just drunk coming back out of her mouth. Wilma gave her a towel and hit her on the back.

"My apologies. How rude. Sorry. But married? I've only been gone a month or so," she said, mortified to have shown herself up in public even among her friends.

"Six weeks, Erin, and we missed you every minute. Why did you take so long?"

They listened as Erin outlined the events of the storm and the aftermath.

"Oh, my goodness, you did have an adventure. Where is Nora now?" Mrs. Grey asked.

"She's at home with Michelle. Both are worn out after the trip," Erin said.

"And what of Lily?"

Erin's eyes shone with pride. "Oh, Wilma, you would not recognize our Lily. She has matured so much. You should have seen her in the hotel. She had the place running so well, the hotel owner offered her a job."

"Our Lily, a hotel manager."

"Yes. Well, for now, but there are other things she is involved in. But tell me about your wedding."

"Where is Alicia? Don't tell me she went home without calling in to see me?"

Erin noticed Wilma avoided the question but decided to play along.

"She has a cold—don't look at me like that. It is just a sniffle but I told her to go home and rest. I wasn't sure how you were after the last time we saw each other. I was just being careful for both your sakes."

"I is fine. I is a tough old bird. You knows that."

The door opened again, admitting an older man. He stopped. Wilma stood and walked to his side.

"This be Zack. Zack, meet Doc Erin."

"Nice to meet you, Doc. My Wilma told me lots about you."

"Nice to meet you too, Zack. I was just about to hear all about you when you interrupted."

Zack laughed. Wilma sent Doc Erin a grateful look for putting her man at ease. He took her seat and helped himself to coffee and cookies.

"As you can see, Doc Erin, he be real shy."

"A working man needs refreshments, woman."

Wilma swiped him gently with her towel. Erin guessed her old friend was hoping to distract people from noticing she was red-faced.

"The short version of the story is this. Zack saved Wilma and her daughter's life a long time ago. They found each other in Denver. Zack found Wilma's granddaughters and came back here when Wilma brought them home," Mrs. Grey explained.

"And your daughter?" Erin asked.

"Solace died a year ago," Wilma replied in a monotone voice.

"Oh, Wilma, I am so sorry."

"What's done is done. At least she was well looked after prior to dying. She didn't die alone and she knew her babies would be safe."

At the closed look on Wilma's face, she decided to ask her another time about Solace.

"So why are they having difficulty settling down here? Do they miss their friends in Denver?" Erin probed.

"They do, but that's not the problem. It's..."

"Charlie Staunton and his cronies. I do wonder if that man ever worries about the time he has to meet his creator," Father Molloy mumbled as he crunched on a cookie.

"It's not just the adults, Father. Bertram Shaw and his friends haven't helped. Eleanor, Laura, and Ellen have taken steps to deal with the school children but it isn't enough," Mrs. Grey added.

"Mick will try to help, too. He has a way of dealing with Bertram," Erin commented.

"Little Beaver has, too. He wanted to let him loose

in the forest for a while to teach him a lesson, but the weather is too cold for that now." Mrs. Grey added, the look on her face suggesting it was never too cold.

"I don't know. I think it might be a good thing but only if you put Staunton, Mrs. Shaw and Ma Kelley with him."

Everyone laughed at Erin's comment.

"It's not just the Clover Springs people behaving badly," Zack added. Wilma glared at him despite acknowledging to Erin before that her grand babies were partly to blame.

"Don't you go looking at me like that, Wilma. You know the truth. Those girls, well they have been through a lot. Heard things, seen things, no child should ever see. Their experiences have left them scarred. It may not be obvious for us to see but they is there all the same. We need to help them to trust themselves, each other and other people."

"You are right as usual, Zack. Being cast out of their family and them losing their ma will have left them feeling insecure," Father Molloy added. "Wilma, don't give me your dirty looks. You can help them heal. We all can. There isn't any point in worrying about what happened and what we could have done differently. We have to move forward. You, the girls and the town."

* * *

Wilma sat back down. Erin took her hand and squeezed it trying to show her solidarity.

"It's hard, Doc. I know they is my flesh and blood but some days I want to thrash them. They can be really hurtful, too."

"That's because they are hurting inside. You can do this, Wilma. Look how many of us you have helped to deal with things we had to overcome. You can do it and we will help. Now, what else have I missed? Any more weddings in the pipeline?"

"Don't start looking at me, Doc. You are barking up the wrong tree. I've been married. That was enough for me," Mrs. Grey responded sharply.

Erin giggled.

"She won't even consider it for me, Erin. She knows how much I love conducting a marriage ceremony." Father Molloy pretended to look upset as he teased Mrs. Grey.

"Don't worry, Father. We brought you some presents from New York. Some packages won't arrive for a few weeks, but we have at least three new couples coming to live in Clover Springs. They all want you to lead the service."

"Three new couples. How exciting," Mrs. Grey exclaimed.

"Yes, and Carmel Doherty and her son and his wife are coming, too. They are just waiting until Joe finishes treatment for his eyes. He went blind in an explosion on the railroad but hopefully, he may regain some sight. Nora will wait until they arrive before she will marry Robbie. Actually, Father if you have time, I should introduce you to Nora and Robbie as soon as possible. Robbie wants to speak to you about converting."

Father Molloy stood up, his face glowing.

"I love being so busy. Let's go meet these new friends of yours, Erin. Wilma and Zack, I need you to let me know what type of ceremony you want."

"They can't get married in the church as Zack has an ex-wife, but Father Molloy said he would do a blessing over them," Lorena Grey explained to Erin.

"He will do anything to get me into his church," joked Wilma.

Erin left the others behind her. She was thrilled to be home but she was feeling tired. The combination of the drama in New York and the long train journey was catching up with her.

CHAPTER 5

Catherine Johnston spotted the priest as he walked down the street chatting amicably to a woman. They seemed like good friends. Father Molloy hadn't changed much. Sure, he had grown older but he was still smiling.

She waited, holding her breath, as he walked by. He didn't seem to recognize her, simply nodded in greeting. She had just breathed a sigh of relief when he was back.

"Excuse me, Ma'am, but you are new to town. Can I be of assistance?"

She tried desperately not to look at his face as she mumbled, "No, thank you, Father."

"Don't I know you? You seem very familiar."

Catherine panicked. “I don’t think so, Father. If you’ll excuse me...”

She picked up her bag and started walking as if she knew where she was going. *Just ask for him help,* the little voice in her head kept saying. But she couldn't. Mary didn’t want to know, she hadn't answered one of her letters. She hadn't given much thought to her sister in later years, thinking she had disowned her. She should have known better. If she closed her eyes, she could see her face at the window as Catherine drove away. Still, family was family, wasn’t it?

“I didn’t mean to intrude, young lady, but I can't help feeling we have met before. The fact you won’t meet my eyes tells me I may be right?”

“Is there something wrong, Father?”

Catherine darted a glance at the other woman. She looked about Mary's age. Maybe she knew her. What harm would it do to ask? But then Father Molloy would recognize her and she wasn’t sure she could deal with his disfavor now.

“Cathy Ryan. It is you, isn't it?”

Now she understood the expression *her stomach landed at her feet,* only hers returned to its rightful place. She thought she would vomit. The street started spinning. She swayed. The woman grabbed her arm.

"Quickly. Father, take her bag. She looks about to faint." The woman took her arm and led her to the boardwalk outside a store, where she forced her to sit down and put her head lower than her body. It was rather undignified, but Cathy couldn't think about that now. Father Molloy had recognized her. There was no escape. She couldn't get back on the train now and disappear. She closed her eyes.

"Doc Erin, you're back. Thought I saw you. Oh, dear, is she alright?"

"Katie, could you get her a glass of water, please. I think she is weak from hunger or maybe she got a fright. She isn't ill. Not from what I can see. No fever, no cough and she doesn't appear to have any spots."

"I am not ill. I just came over funny. I will be all right in a minute or two." Katie? It couldn't be Katie O'Callaghan. At this rate, she would meet everyone before Mary.

She struggled to sit up, reassuring the doctor she was fine. Katie returned with the glass.

"Thank you, Katie."

"You're wel.... How did you know my name?" Katie asked, looking at her. "Cathy? Cathy Ryan. Oh, thank God you're alive. We thought you were dead. Wait until Mary sees you. She will be so happy."

Cathy looked at her sister's best friend and started to cry. She couldn't help it. The guilt was eating her up inside.

"I am so sorry. Tell her I am sorry." And then she passed out in the blackness.

CHAPTER 6

Abe O'Malley walked down the street from the saloon. Gary Barrett had kindly given him a job. It was thanks to Cookie. He'd been lucky Cookie was able to give him a roof over his head for the first few days. He had tried to get him work, too, but although Davy Sullivan and his wife Mary, were very kind, they didn't need any more hands at the time. Luckily, the position at the saloon had come up or he would have had more problems.

He hadn't anticipated Mick not being in Clover Springs when he got here. Especially as he had telegraphed Doc Deane to say he'd got married to some doctor and planned on staying in Clover Springs full time. He'd even sold his farm out in Virginia, something they thought he'd never do. Cookie had left for Noelle the day after he arrived.

He had locked the saloon after cleaning it thoroughly. Gary was busy working on his new house on a plot beside the school. He had asked Abe to help him with the building work, but first to close up the saloon and drop by the mercantile to buy some of Mrs. Higgins's fine cookies. She had started supplying the store fairly regularly, given the high demand by the men for some home cooked foods. As he turned the corner, he saw the woman stretched out on the boardwalk, a priest and two women fussing over her. He moved to help.

"Can I do anything to help, ma'am? Abe O'Malley is my name. I help Gary out at the saloon."

"Thank you, Abe. Could you carry her to my office. I am Doc Erin. I need to examine her properly." Abe was about to say he knew her husband but the other woman spoke first.

"Father Molloy, can you mind the store until Daniel gets back? He will only be a few minutes. I want to go and find Mary. She needs to come to town."

"Be happy to, Katie. Be gentle telling Mary."

Abe picked up the young woman. She was feather light, as if she hadn't eaten for some time. She was very pale. He cradled her close like you would a child.

Only she didn't smell like a child. She smelled of lavender and freshness as well as a scent that was unmistakably hers.

Looking at her, he didn't see her face but that of another woman. He followed the doctor to her office. It wasn't far—not that it mattered. He was used to carrying heavier loads than this lady.

He lay the woman out on the table the doc indicated and withdrew from the room to give them some privacy. He figured he'd better wait a few minutes in case the lady doc needed him to go for anyone else. He wondered where Mick was. On one hand, he couldn't wait to see him, but on the other, he knew his news was upsetting. He frowned, his mind on the past year.

CHAPTER 7

The door behind him opened. Doc Erin came out, drying her hands with a cloth. "Thank you so much, Abe. We are lucky you came along when you did. Father Molloy is too old to be carrying anyone, only don't tell him I said that."

Abe nodded. "Will the woman be all right?"

Doc Erin's face creased up slightly. She looked not worried but perplexed. "I believe so. I will know more when I find out her story. Some of the residents recognized her, but I haven't been living here all that long. I don't know her, although she looks a little familiar. "

"Do you need anything else, Doc? Can I get anyone for you?"

"No, thank you, Abe. Emer Shipley, the town nurse,

will be back any minute. I think Doc may be out on a tour of some of the outlying ranches, although given our recent weather, I hope he didn't go too far. Anyway, I best let you get back. I hope I didn't delay you too much."

"No, you didn't. I was just going to buy Gary some cookies from the mercantile. I will see you around, Mrs. Quinn."

Abe was gone before he realized what he had called her. Maybe she hadn't picked up on it. He should have said he was looking for Mick. He walked back to the store, wondering if the priest was still there. He was, sitting behind the counter, munching and enjoying a cookie. His face flushed as Abe opened the door. He looked like a child caught doing something he shouldn't.

"Ah, you're the fine young man who came to our aid earlier. I was worried you were Katie."

"Why?"

"She wouldn't be happy with me."

"Eating her profits?" Abe asked, thinking that was a little mean especially as he was minding the store.

"No, son. Katie O'Sullivan wouldn't mind. She'd give you the shirt off her back."

The confusion must have shown on his face as the priest laughed and tapped his belly.

"This is the reason she would be mad. Doc Erin told me off for eating too many cakes and she told the women of the town not to feed me. Katie and some of the other ladies took her too literally. She didn't mean me to never eat another cookie. Life is too short not to have a little fun, don't you think?"

Life was way too short. Shorter than you ever imagined. He turned on his heel and left as the walls of the store started to move in on top of him. His breathing got ragged and his hands started sweating. He tried to breathe just as Doc Deane had shown him. Slowly. Breathe in, breathe out slowly. Count to ten. Do it again. Gradually his heart stopped racing. The blackness around his eyes receded to find the priest staring at him, a glass of water in his hand. "Not sure what is wrong with the air in Clover Springs today but it seems to be badly affecting you young'uns. Anything I can do to help, son?"

"No, Father. Sorry about before. I didn't mean to be rude. I get these funny turns. Have to get outdoors."

"No offense taken, lad. I am always around if you need to talk. With a name like O'Malley, you have to be from the same place I am."

The store bell tinkled, making the priest stand straighter. "I best get back. Don't want to be caught slacking in my new position."

Abe grinned as the priest walked smartly back into the store. He was a nice man. Pity he couldn't do anything to help him. Abe wasn't interested in God or religion. He used to believe, and look where that had got him. No, from now on it was just him. And that's the way it was going to stay.

CHAPTER 8

An unfamiliar smell wafting under her nose, turning her stomach, woke Catherine up. Where was she? In some sort of doctor's office, judging by the cabinets on the walls. She moved to get off the bed when a wave of dizziness hit her again.

"Move slowly...that's better. Now you won't get as lightheaded. When did you last eat?"

The woman in front of her wasn't the same woman who had been with the priest. Panic gripped her. Was it true? Was she mad? Had they locked her up?

"Where am I?"

"In the doctor's office. Doc Erin brought you in. You've been asleep for a while. My name is Emer. I am one of the nurses here."

"Is it a lunatic asylum?"

The woman called Emer gave her a funny look. "No. Cathy, isn't that your name?"

"Catherine. Catherine Johnston."

The woman looked confused. "I thought Doc Erin said you were Cathy Ryan. She must be exhausted from her trip."

"My sister always called me Cathy. Mama didn't like it. But I do."

The lady smiled. "Cathy, this is the doctor's office. There are no asylums here. You are safe."

She was wrong. She was never going to safe. Not again. They would come for her. They had promised. She'd been lucky, but luck always ran out. Her ma hadn't been lucky coming over from Ireland. Ironic, really, her adoptive parents suffering the same fate. Yet she'd escaped, both times. Was it true? Was she cursed?

"Cathy, can you eat something for me? Doc thinks you are getting lightheaded due to hunger."

She was starving but she couldn't eat. What if it was poisoned? Then she would have those dreams again where she couldn't move her arms, her legs.

She shook her head. She didn't want food but she was thirsty. "I'd like some water please."

The door opened. Cathy shrunk back on the bed but it was only Doc Erin. She looked back at Emer, who was staring at her in concern. She grasped the glass of water and drank it greedily.

"Cathy, drink slowly or you will be sick. That's it. Smaller sips. Good girl."

Cathy kept taking small sips as the two women moved into the other room. She could barely hear their conversation, but she heard the word asylum and concern. She closed her eyes. Where was Mary? Was she not coming? Could she blame her if she didn't? It was a bit much to walk back into someone's life all these years later.

She heard the commotion outside the door. A woman was crying. She let the glass fall. It couldn't be happening again. No. No.

"Cathy, shush, love. Nothing is going to happen to you, nothing will hurt you. You are safe here. Listen to me. I won't let anyone near you, I promise." Doc Erin was almost cuddling her. She wished she could stop shaking.

"You swear?" Her voice was as shaky as the rest of her. She was holding the doctor too tightly. She'd leave marks on her wrist. But her hands wouldn't respond to her command to loosen. What was wrong with her? Was she losing her mind after all? Archibald was right. She was cursed.

"Cathy—or would you prefer Catherine—I

promise you as your doctor you are safe. I won't let anyone see you unless you want to see them. Now, can you loosen your grip or I will have to ask Emer to strap up my broken wrist."

She stared into the doctor's face—she was smiling, her expression reassuring. She lessened her hold. "Cathy. That's what my sister called me."

"Cathy it is, then. Now, please lie back on the pillow. I am going to give you something to help you relax."

She shook her head. She didn't want anything. That was what had got her into this mess in the first place. Archibald had promised it would help stop the nightmares and it had at first, but then they had come back worse than ever.

She shook her head violently. She had given in on the train but she had to stop taking it.

"Okay, Cathy. I won't give you anything but you need to lie back and try to relax. I am going out to tell Katie and the rest to go away. I will be back in to see you then."

"You won't let them in, will you?"

"No, I won't."

"You promise?"

"Cathy, I promise. I know you have just met me but

try to trust me. Nothing will happen to you. Emer is going to wait with you. We won't leave you alone."

She glanced at Emer, who also smiled at her. She looked nice. Could she trust her? She heard the voice outside. Could she afford not to?

She closed her eyes and nodded. Erin let her go gently and then moved to the door. She watched her go. The doctor shut the door firmly behind her, leaving her alone with Emer.

"Try to rest, Cathy. I don't know what happened to you before you came here, but you are safe now. I promise."

She wiped the tears from her eyes. She wanted to believe that but she had done that before. Trusted someone, and look where that got her.

CHAPTER 9

Abe told Gary that Mick and Erin were back in town. He didn't mention the woman he'd carried, thinking she wouldn't want people to know she had fainted. How was she? He hoped she'd get well soon. From what she weighed in his arms, she needed a few good meals. Her face had been familiar but he was sure he hadn't met her before. He had only been in Clover Springs a few weeks, spending most of that time helping by doing Cookie's share of chores on the Sullivan ranch. Cookie had taken off for Noelle as soon as Abe had told him of the troubles facing Doc Deane.

Mary Sullivan. That's who the woman reminded him of. But she didn't have any close relatives living in Clover Springs. She hadn't mentioned any sisters, yet she spoke about Katie, the lady who owned the mercantile, quite a bit. Katie was Mary's sister-in-law. He hoped the lady would be okay. He could feel her fear, her body shaking, see the terror in her eyes. He thought first she was scared of men, maybe someone had done something to her. But she seemed equally scared of Doc Erin. Still, he had work to do. He didn't have time to stand around thinking about a strange woman.

"So it's true? Abe O'Malley. It's great to see you but what brought you down this way?" Mick Quinn's voice brought him out of his daydreaming.

"That's a lovely welcome. Along the lines of nice to see you but when are you going home?" Gary replied to Mick's comment, making them both laugh.

He didn't laugh. He stared at Mick, wishing he'd rehearsed what he was going to say. But seeing Mick brought everything rushing back. The last time Mick had been in Noelle, Sally was expecting the baby.

"So where's the missus and your baby? Must be coming up on two now, I reckon. Where do the years go?"

"Ain't you got a note yet?" he asked, playing for time.

"Note from who? I ain't even seen Cookie yet. Not got a chance to get out to the Sullivan ranch. Every time I head out that way, someone stops me and sends me somewhere else. How is the old coot?"

"He's fine."

"Abe, why don't you take a break? Go have a drink with Mick," Gary suggested, throwing him the keys to the saloon.

"It's a bit early, ain't it?" Mick protested.

"Nope, you been away a while. You need to get caught up on everyone's news."

He swallowed hard as Gary gave Mick a look that told his friend to shut up and go for the drink. He didn't look at Mick but put his tools down near Gary and set off for the saloon in silence. Mick walked with him but thankfully took the hint.

He opened the saloon, allowed Mick in and then locked the door behind him. He didn't want any interruptions.

"Okay, you're scaring me now. What's going on? Is Cookie alright?"

"Cookie is fine. He's gone to Noelle. Doc Deane needs a friend."

"Doc? Why? Abe, what the heck is going on?"

He poured two shots of whiskey and gave one to Mick. He downed the other one and refilled it just as quick.

"What are you doing? You of all people know there's no help at the bottom of the bottle."

"Yeah, well, maybe you're wrong and pa was right. It helps dull the pain."

"Abe O'Malley, put that bottle down and tell me what on earth is going on."

"Sally's dead, so is the babe. Lots of people died. Doc Deane couldn't save them." He threw the glass against the wall, the frustration getting to him. The tears pooled behind his eyes and he angrily wiped them away. Then he picked up the bottle. Mick had it out of his hands in seconds.

"Sit down and start from the beginning."

He gave himself a few minutes to compose his thoughts and then tried to speak. It took a couple of attempts but finally he was able to talk without blubbering like a baby.

"About a year ago, a couple of miners came in, coughing and spluttering. Doc thought it might be serious and he put them in quarantine, only some didn't listen. Sally's Pa was one of them. He got sick and she, being the only girl, went to help her ma look after him. I warned her not to. She was weak after having the baby. But she didn't listen. Why don't people listen?"

"What happened next, Abe?"

"What do you think happened?" he screamed back. "They died. All of them. Sally, the babe, her ma, pa, everyone. Ma and my sister Cara got sick but they recovered, thanks to Doc Deane, but he isn't well, Mick. He blames himself. His missus and young'uns are walking around him as if they are walking on egg shells."

"Abe, I'm sorry about Sally and your child. She was a nice girl."

"She was. What did she ever do to anyone? Nothing. Yet she died before she was even twenty. What type of God lets that happen?"

Mick didn't answer him, but he reckoned that was probably a good thing. If anyone else told him God had a plan and his own reasons for doing things, he reckoned he would hit them. Hard.

"Did you tell Cookie this?"

"Yes, sir. He rode out the following morning."

"Why didn't he tell me? Send me a telegram?"

"Cookie said not to. He said you had plenty enough troubles in New York, otherwise you would have come back. He left you a note but you obviously didn't get it."

"I wish he had told me. Did he go alone?"

"Yes, he did. He wanted me to go with him but I ain't never going back there. I stayed long enough to get the ground cleared and ready for sale. I stocked up Ma's larder and got her place as good as I could. The boys can help her now. I am done with that place. I am heading East. Going to try New York."

"Why don't you wait a bit? You have a job here and we have some friends coming from New York. They can tell you more about the city and then you can decide what you want to do."

"I think it's best if I head out soon. I just wanted to be here to tell you in person."

"I am real glad you did but Abe, don't make any sudden decisions. I have never lost a child but I have lost people I loved. Now is the time to be near friends."

He looked up at Mick, ashamed at the tears on his face but unable to stop them.

"Don't know if I can do that Mick. My life is over. I ain't got any reasons for carrying on."

Mick didn't react as he expected. He didn't get the hand on the shoulder or any sympathy. Instead, Mick got angry.

"That's enough of that self-pity. Talking like that never got anyone anywhere. You are staying in Clover Springs for at least the next month and that's final. I am not about to let you go do something stupid. Doc Deane would kill me and if he didn't, your ma would."

His ma. He didn't want to think about her. He'd left

her alone. Her and Cara. His brothers were around but would they call in now he wasn't home? He wasn't sure. Since pa had died, he'd been the man of the house. He'd been the one to make them do chores and school work. As soon as they were old enough, all of them had left.

"Your ma worked her socks off to keep you all fed and clothed and protected when your pa was alive. How many times did she stand between his fist and you, Abe O'Malley?"

"What's that supposed to mean? I was a kid back then. What was I to do?"

"But you're not a kid anymore. Don't you dare go doing something stupid and bring more pain to your ma. She's had enough of that to last a lifetime. You hear me?"

"Yes, sir."

He saw Mick clench his fists at the tone he'd used but he didn't strike out. In a way, Abe wished he had. He needed to punch someone. Oh, what was he thinking? Mick had never been anything but a friend to him. Like a big brother. There wasn't the age gap between them that had been between him and Cookie or Doc.

"Sorry, Mick. That wasn't called for."

"Don't worry about it. But Abe, I want you to stay in town. Just for a bit. Promise me?"

"Okay."

"Come on, let's get out of here. I can introduce you to my missus."

Abe cleared up the mess on the floor. "I met her already. Had to carry a patient for her. Some woman collapsed on the street. Mrs. Quinn seems like a nice woman."

"She is and a great doctor, but don't go calling her missus, not if you want to get on her good side. It's Doc Erin." Mick looked around the saloon. "Right. Let's get home, then. I can introduce you to Nora and Robbie. Both of them are from New York. They may tell you enough stories to put you off venturing East."

He doubted it, but he wasn't about to say so.

CHAPTER 10

Erin looked up as Mary Sullivan ran into her office.

"Is it true? You have my sister lying in that room?" Mary probably didn't mean to sound accusatory. Erin guessed she was finding it hard to believe her sister had turned up today, after all these years.

"Mary, please come outside. We need to talk but I don't want to upset my patient."

Mary stared at Doc Erin, an expression of disbelief on her face. "Erin, my sister in on the other side of that door and you want me to go out to the street. What is wrong with Cathy? I don't care if my little sister is contagious. I haven't seen her in years. She must need me. She came here."

"Mary, outside now. Doc Erin knows best. Come on, now."

Mary allowed Mrs. Grey to lead her from the office outside onto the porch. She sat in the chair Mrs. Grey indicated.

Erin sat beside her, taking her hand. "Mary, I am sorry, but I can't allow you to see Cathy at the moment. She doesn't want to see anyone."

"But she came here to Clover Springs. Why else would she come here?" Mary replied.

"She probably did come to see you if she is your sister."

"What do you mean if? Now, listen here, Erin Quinn, I'd know my own sister."

"Mary, love, calm down. Erin is trying to help. It is Cathy." Katie crouched down and held her hands. "I recognized her but for some reason, Cathy doesn't want to face you yet."

"But she's my family, Katie, my own flesh and blood. Why wouldn't she want to see me?" Mary's voice shook.

Erin couldn't imagine how she was feeling. Knowing your sister who had been missing for years was within arm's distance, yet being prevented from seeing her.

"Mary, it seems Cathy is in trouble. I don't know

what type of trouble, but she is quite fragile. And very scared," Erin said quietly.

"Oh, the poor darling. What happened to her, Doc?" Mary put her hand to her mouth.

"I don't know. I can't see any form of obvious mistreatment, apart from the fact she hasn't eaten for some time. She will only drink water. She seems…"

Mary waited for Doc to finish what she was saying. Erin stayed silent for a few seconds, trying to choose the correct word. She didn't want to scare Mary, yet she had to give her a believable explanation. "Nervous."

"Oh, dear God, what have they done to her? They seemed like nice people. Stuck up and rich, but I thought they cared about her. What did they do?"

"Mary, calm down. You aren't doing yourself or your sister any good getting into a state. I will help you but my priority has to be my patient. Perhaps, Katie, you could take Mary back to your mother-in-law's. She could make her a cup of tea and let her stay. That way you will be nearby when Cathy is ready to talk."

"Will you ask her again, Doc? I know you are doing your best. But see, I haven't seen her in a long time. So long I thought she was dead."

"Mary, you have my word. I will do my best. But

for now, I have to go back to her. I have to prove to her she can trust me." Erin hated herself for hurting Mary but for the moment, Cathy had to be the priority.

She watched as Mary blessed herself before heading off in the direction of Martha Sullivan's guesthouse. Her mother-in-law would mind Mary's children. She loved having them around her.

CHAPTER 11

Later, Erin called to Martha's house to bring Mary up to date about Cathy.

"Can Mary see Cathy?" Martha asked.

Erin shook her head, but before she could explain, Mary started talking.

"Erin said Cathy was scared, Ma. Why on earth would Cathy be afraid of me?"

"Maybe she is worried you will reject her, love. It's been years and she never contacted you. All those letters you wrote and she just ignored them."

"Why would I do that? I love her. She's my baby sister. All I have left."

Martha put her arms around Mary and hugged her closer. "She was all you had left. You have us now. Davy loves the bones of ye and those fine children."

Martha took a breath. “So much time has passed since you last saw each other, a couple of days won’t make any difference.”

“It might not take that long Mary. We have to be patient.”

“I don’t know what she is feeling, but give it time. Even when the two of you meet, you will have to take things slow.” Martha still held Mary close. “People change, Mary. You have changed so much since you first arrived in Clover Springs. There was a time you wouldn’t say boo to a goose.”

“They were the good times, Ma, weren’t they?” Katie teased. “Daniel’s looking after the shop. I thought you might need a hug. And I could murder a cup of tea.”

“Oh, Katie, where would I be without your support. You were there at the very start of this. Cathy can’t be afraid of me, can she?”

Erin exchanged a glance with Katie.

“I think you better be prepared, Mary. Something happened to Cathy and whatever it was has her running scared.” Katie paused. “The look of terror in her eyes was frightening. We need to do everything Doc says. If we don’t, you may drive Cathy away forever.”

"I will never be separated from my sister again. Never."

"Mary, do you know anything about the people who adopted Cathy? Why would she be traveling alone? What brought her to Clover Springs now, after all these years?"

"No, Doc, I haven't any idea. I wrote to Cathy but never heard anything back. The last time I saw my sister, she was driving away with a couple called Johnston. They were adopting her but only wanted one child."

"I need to find out more, but at the moment Cathy appears too scared to talk." At the look on Mary's face, Erin continued. "I am certain she came here looking for you, Mary. So be brave for a little while longer. I best get back to the office."

"Thank you, Erin. You look tired, so don't forget to look after yourself as well."

"You too, Mary."

* * *

ERIN CLOSED the door behind her. What on earth could have happened to Cathy to leave the girl in such a state? She had no bruising or any other injuries consistent with force so it hadn't been physical. But something had the girl running scared.

"Good evening, Doctor. I was wondering if my wife was coming home at all today?"

Erin looked up with a smile at Mick. He was teasing her, but she saw the concern in his eyes.

"I have a new patient. I need to stay here."

"Erin, you need to rest. You are tired out. I am sure Mrs. Grey and Emer can cope. Where is Doc?"

"He hasn't come back to town yet. We think he might be holed up on an outlying ranch."

"Probably. But now I am going to insist you come home with me. You are exhausted. Michelle needs a cuddle from her ma and Nora is probably feeling a bit lost."

Nora! She hadn't given her poor friend a second thought, although she was with Robbie so she would be fine.

"Go on, Erin, we can look after Cathy. Come back in the morning. You will do better after a night's sleep."

Erin gave in. She was over-tired and that wouldn't help anyone. Taking Mick's arm, she let him walk her home.

"How did you get on with the twins today?"

"They are little rascals. Bertram is smitten with

Amy, keeps giving her flowers. Poor boy can't see that his hatred of her twin is never going to endear him."

"Poor boy? This is Bertram Shaw you are talking about."

"Yes, Erin, but in this instance, I think he has more than met his match. Wilma's girls have been making his life miserable. Even Eleanor is feeling sorry for him."

Erin couldn't believe what she was hearing. Suzy and Amy seemed like such sweet little creatures.

"It will all come to blows shortly, I reckon."

"After all the trouble that boy has caused, he deserves what's coming to him."

"That ain't very Christian, now, is it, Doc?"

"Stop teasing me, Mick. I need a hug not teasing."

He took her in his arms and kissed the top of her head. "Sorry, darling. Bad day at work?"

"Mary's sister, Cathy, showed up. She is in a bad way. Terrified of something, but we don't know what. She came miles – at least by the look of her she has traveled a long distance, although we don't know where she came from – to see her sister and now refuses to do just that."

They'd reached their house. Pushing open the door, they were greeted by the delicious aroma of a cooked meal.

"Looks like Nora has settled in just fine," Mick said, sniffing the air appreciatively."

They walked into the kitchen to find the table set. Robbie had Michelle on his lap and Nora was tending to the stove.

"Isn't this the picture of domestic bliss?" Mick teased, making Robbie smile. Erin caught Nora's look of concern but smiled back, hoping to offset her fears. She would be fine after a good night's sleep.

* * *

"ERIN, this is Abe O'Malley. Cookie and I met Abe when he was fifteen, quite a few years ago. I believe you two met already."

"Nice to meet you, Abe. Thank you for your help earlier."

"T'was nothin', Mrs. Quinn. Sorry, I mean Doc Erin."

Erin smiled to try to put him at ease. "I see my husband has been coaching you on what to call me."

"He said you got a bit rattled if people called you missus."

"Oh, he did, did he?" Erin said making a point of staring at Mick.

"Now, that's just lovely, Abe. Thanks a lot for

getting me in trouble with my missus. Maybe I should make you stay in the saloon after all."

"I already said I was fine over there," Abe retorted.

"Abe, you are welcome to stay here. Mick is only teasing. Robbie might welcome some company of his own age."

"Ah, now, that's just lovely. Now my missus is calling me old."

Everyone laughed. Erin took Michelle onto her lap and cuddled her. But despite the warmth of the people around her, she couldn't get her mind off her new patient.

CHAPTER 12

She opened her eyes to find Doc Erin sitting at her side. The doctor seemed to be sleeping. She moved slightly, causing the doc to open her eyes and smile.

"I am just back from New York, Cathy, and still a bit tired. Sorry about that," Erin said.

She was being very nice to her. Could she be trusted?

"Would you like a drink? Something to eat?"

"Some water, please," she said.

Erin poured her water and gave it to her with instructions to drink it slowly.

"Cathy, can you try to eat something for me. The longer you leave it the harder it will be. I can get you anything you want, well within reason. I don't think your stomach could handle a steak right now."

She smiled. Erin was making a huge effort to make her feel safe. "An apple?"

Erin said she would see what she could do. She left, leaving her alone with her thoughts. Had anyone followed her? Did they know where she was? She closed her eyes again. She was so tired. Her mind focused on a kind face with eyes so brown, they seemed black. He had smiled at her and for some unknown reason, she'd felt safe in his arms. He was a complete stranger, this brown-eyed man.

"Cathy, wake up. I got your apple. I sliced it up for you," Erin said, handing her the plate.

She bit her lip, wishing the apple was whole, then she could check it for marks. Sliced up meant anything could be hidden inside. She looked from the plate to Erin and back.

"What?"

"Nothing," she said.

"Cathy, tell me. Why are you scared of eating?"

She picked at the cover on the bed. She was starving, yet scared. Could she risk it?

"Cathy?"

"I think that's how they gave me the stuff." There it was, out in the open.

"What stuff?" Erin looked perplexed, then her eyes cleared. "Do you mean you were drugged?"

She nodded.

"Oh, dear God. No wonder you won't eat or drink anything, only water. I swear, it's just an apple. See?" Erin took a couple of slices and ate them.

She picked up the thinnest slice and put it into her mouth. It tasted divine and just how an apple should taste. There was no bitter aftertaste. She took a couple more slices before her stomach protested.

"Take things slowly. Your stomach will cooperate better if you have regular small meals rather than trying to eat a lot now. What other things would you like?"

Erin listed off items of food to try and tempt her appetite, but she really didn't care what she ate. She asked the question she was dreading the answer to. She wanted her here and not here at the same time.

"Is Mary here?"

Erin nodded. "She is staying at her mother-in-law's house nearby. She has visited a few times. She brought a book and some cookies. She wanted to take your bag to sort out your clothes, do your laundry and all that, but I said no. Did I do the right thing?"

"Yes, thank you. Although she might understand a little if she opened the bag."

"Will I get it for you?"

She smiled her thanks as Erin produced the bag. She opened it and took the small bundle out of it. Without a word, she handed it to Erin.

"These are letters. Lots of letters?" Erin's confusion mirrored hers when she had first found the bundle.

"They are Mary's letters to me."

"You kept them after all these years."

"I never saw them. At least not until a few months ago. My parents, the people who adopted me, hid them from me. My letters to Mary are in the bag."

Erin stared at the letters and then back at her.

"You mean you never got them and the ones you wrote were never posted? But why?"

"I don't know." And she didn't. No matter how many times she had asked herself that question, she couldn't find an answer. Her parents hadn't been cruel. Yes, they were over-protective and appeared terrified something would happen to her. She'd thought that was because their own children—a boy and a girl had died before they adopted her. But maybe it was more than that. She couldn't put her thoughts into words. Then Erin would think she belonged in the asylum Archibald had threatened her with.

"Oh, you poor thing. What did your parents say when you found them? Or is that why you ran away?"

"My parents died six months ago. In a boating accident. I was thrown clear and rescued. I found them when I was in my mother's bedroom. It was one place I wasn't allowed to be alone in when she was alive." she corrected herself quickly as it sounded like she had been snooping. "I went to her room because I missed her so much. I wanted to feel her presence. I put on some of her favorite clothes and scent, thinking it might bring her closer. And then I found those. All neat and tidy, wrapped in two bows. She liked to keep things tidy."

She hated the bitterness in her voice but she couldn't help blaming her mother. Why had she kept the letters from her? All those years, she thought Mary hated her for being adopted. Hated her for having a better station in life, a beautiful home, everything she could possibly want. But she had wanted Mary so badly. She had begged her parents over and over to adopt Mary, too, but they wouldn't. They did everything else to keep her happy—buying her a puppy and a horse and every other gift a girl would love. But she'd wanted her sister. From reading her letters, she knew now Mary had wanted her just as badly. Or she had. The words on the last letter Mary had sent were clear as day in her mind.

This will be the last letter I write, my darling sister. I keep hoping for news of you but you have obviously moved on. Davy, my husband, says its time to close the door on the past. Time to put the hurt to bed. I love you, Cathy and hope you are happy. Goodbye.

Erin sat in silence. She appreciated the fact that she didn't ask questions but seemed to be waiting for her to say something.

"I guess you think I am rather sad for carrying them around with me."

"I don't think that at all. I think it's sad two sisters were kept apart for so many years. Emer, our nurse, has some experience of a similar thing happening. She can tell you about it one day. I believe your mother had her reasons. From what you have said, they showed you love in other ways. Nobody teaches you how to be a good parent, you just muddle along and do your best."

She lay back on the pillow. Was that right? Had her parents really loved her? She didn't know what to believe now. She was tired. So tired.

"Cathy, sleep is the best thing for you right now. The loss of your parents combined with everything else will have taken its toll on your body. Would you like me to give these to Mary?"

She sat up a little. She didn't know. Was it a good idea?

"It may help her understand. And it would help you if she knew. Save you the energy of explaining," Erin added.

That was a good idea. Mary could read for herself and know she hadn't forgotten her. Maybe then she would forgive her for leaving?

"Please do, Doc Erin. Thank you."

"You're welcome, Cathy. Now rest. When you wake up, we can try one of Mary's cookies. I heard Mrs. Higgins has been teaching her how to bake cookies. Funny how she's lived in Clover Springs with one of the best cooks in the town and she has yet to master cookies. Let's see how well the lessons worked."

She closed her eyes, smiling. Doc had a way of making her feel better. Maybe it was time for everything to turn out well now.

CHAPTER 13

Erin asked Katie to come to see Mary with her. What was coming was likely to be a big shock.

"Is it Cathy? Is she worse?"

"No, Mary. In fact, Cathy is a little better." Erin tried to pick the right words. "Mary, you need to sit down and prepare yourself for some bad news. Cathy is fine—at least, she will be. But she has something to share with you. I asked Katie to be with us in case you need someone else apart from Martha."

Quickly, Erin told the ladies about Cathy's parents dying in a boating accident over six months ago and how she had been the sole survivor. Cathy had very few memories of the accident. She couldn't really remember what she was doing on a boat, as she hated the water.

"Not again. Our parents died on the way over here. Cathy was terrified of the water."

"Unfortunately, the loss of her parents isn't the only thing Cathy had to deal with. Mary, your sister wrote to you regularly."

Mary stared at her in confusion. "But I never got a letter. I wrote to her all the time but nothing ever came back. Eventually, Davy told me it would be best to stop writing. He was trying to protect me. I thought she didn't care." Mary sobbed.

"She thought the same."

Mary's head lifted. "What? But how? I sent the letters to the address the convent gave me. Oh, if that Mother Superior—she couldn't be that mean, could she?"

"We all know she was a complete witch, Mary. Look how she treated Ben and Sorcha. She could have done anything," Katie said, taking Mary's hand.

"I don't know this nun, but it wasn't her fault. Cathy's adoptive mother kept the letters. She kept both sets, those Cathy wrote and those you sent her. I have them here." Erin laid the two bundles of letters on the table. The writing on one set of envelopes was obviously written by a child.

"She wrote?" Mary looked at the letters, obviously not wanting to touch them.

Erin couldn't blame her. Opening them would bring back all sorts of memories.

"All these years, I thought she didn't care but she did. Why would her mother do this?"

"That's something I can't answer. Now I must get back to Cathy."

"Can I come with you?"

"I think it would be best for you to read the letters first, Mary. I will speak to Cathy and maybe she will see you tomorrow. She has started eating a little bit so she is building her strength up."

"Thank you, Doc, for looking after Cathy so well. I will look after Mary. We will see you tomorrow."

Martha walked Erin out to the front door and pulled it almost shut behind her.

"There is something you are not telling Mary, isn't there, Doc?"

Erin knew Martha was a caring, trustworthy lady but there was no way she could tell her anything. What Cathy had said—or, more specifically, hinted at —had to stay between her and her patient.

"All I can say, Martha, is Mary is lucky to have you. She will need your support over the next few weeks. If you need me for any reason, send someone."

"I will, Doc. Now you take care of yourself. You look tired, too, if you don't mind me saying."

Erin smiled and left. She wished she could rest but she had patients to see and wanted to check on Wilma. Although the older woman seemed fine, those turns she had prior to Erin going to New York had been worrying.

CHAPTER 14

Wilma and Father Molloy arrived at Erin's house just as she got home. Wilma was carrying a large basket. From the smell, Erin guessed it was enough food to feed them for a week.

"Erin, you look very tired. Are you running yourself ragged? Mrs. Grey and Emer looked after everything very nicely when you were away."

"Yes, they did, and I appreciate it. I am just a bit worried about my new patient."

"I came to talk to you about that. Would it help if I came to visit her? I knew Cathy Ryan when she was younger. Never did agree with the adoption but the Mother Superior was a force to be reckoned with. I might be able to offer young Cathy some comfort."

"That would be wonderful, Father, but aren't you a little busy, too? Robbie says you two have started working on his conversion. You are planning Nora's wedding, Sadie and Lizzie will be here soon and will want to get married and you have—"

"Erin, will you stop or you will have me dying of exhaustion?" Father Molloy asked, smiling. "You know me. I am happier when I am busy. Anyway, in your long list, you forgot about one major event."

Erin stared at him, her mind blank.

"Wilma?"

"Me and Zack agreed to be married. We want to have a big party and hoped you would be there with us to celebrate."

"Oh, Wilma, that's wonderful. Of course I will be there. Wild horses couldn't stop me. When is it?"

"We thought we would have it in three weeks' time. We had to cancel the last party we were planning because I got ill and then you guys had to go to New York. This time, hopefully there will be no surprises."

"Wouldn't bet on that, Wilma. This is Clover Springs. We always get surprises."

"Most of the time they are good ones, though," Erin said, crossing her fingers that Cathy's arrival would turn out to be a blessing rather than a curse.

"When is the sheriff coming back?"

"I didn't know he was away, Wilma. Little Beaver didn't say anything."

"He is keeping it quiet, as you know how some resent him being in charge. Sheriff had to go up to Leadville. They got some trouble up there. He should be back in time for the wedding, though."

"I didn't know you were very friendly with him. I mean, he is a nice man, but…" Erin looked at Wilma, certain she was missing something.

"I think Wilma is doing some match-making Erin. She seems to think Mrs. Grey and our sheriff would make a good match."

"Really? Funny, I can't see that. Mrs. Grey is always so proper and, well, Sheriff isn't used to dealing with the more genteel elements." Erin smiled before she added, "You are just all romantic and think everyone else should be too, Wilma. Mrs. Grey seems quite happy on her own."

"I don't know, Erin. I think Wilma may be right. Mrs. Grey might be a little lonely," Father Molloy said, helping himself to more cake.

"Father Molloy, what happened to cutting down on sweet things?"

"Doc Erin, are you planning another trip soon? I quite liked being able to eat in peace."

Erin laughed as the priest teased her. They chatted for a while more and then after her guests left, Erin changed. She had to go back to check on her patients.

CHAPTER 15

"Doc Erin, could I see the man who carried me here? I would like to say thank you."

"Who? Abe? He is staying with us at the moment. I will ask him to call in after he is finished helping Gary."

"Have you known him long?" She stared at the bed covers, not fully understanding why she wanted to know more about the man. He intrigued her. He had kind eyes but they were full of sadness, too.

"No, he's a friend of my husband's. He suffered a tragedy recently and came to Clover Springs for a bit. He says he is moving on soon enough."

She didn't reply. She wondered what type of tragedy but she wasn't about to ask Erin. From the little she knew of the doc, she wasn't one for gossip.

* * *

Later that afternoon, there was a knock on the door and the tall man with the brown eyes popped his head around the door.

"Doc said you waned to see me, ma'am"

"Yes, please come in. Thank you for coming. I wanted to say thank you for the other day. For coming to my rescue."

"You're welcome, but I didn't do anything special. You look better."

She looked down at the dress she was wearing. Once, it had fit her properly. Now it hung loosely. She had lost too much weight. He was being kind.

"I feel it, thank you."

"Well, I best be going."

"Thank you, Abe."

He put his hat back on and was gone. She sat there, staring after him. What was it about him that made her pulse race faster? She wanted to get to know him better. Silly, really. He was a total stranger and from what Erin had said, he wouldn't be around town for all that long.

* * *

"Did Abe call in? Has he gone already? I wanted him to take a message home for me."

"You can go home, Doc. I don't need watching. I am much better now."

She saw the doctor hesitate. "Don't worry, I wont steal your drugs." She immediately regretted being so straight as the doctor flushed.

"When did you start taking opium, Cathy?"

"I don't know exactly. I found it hard to deal with Papa and Mama dying. Archibald, he's my cousin of sorts, suggested calling a doctor. The doctor said it would help to dull the pain."

From the expression on Doc's face, she guessed Erin wasn't impressed.

"The doc said not to take too much. He gave the bottle to Archibald and told him someone was to give me a few drops each morning. I think he meant the housekeeper or something. It would not be appropriate for Archibald to be in my bedroom in the mornings. Not until we were married."

"You were to marry your cousin?"

"Yes, he's not really my cousin. I was adopted. I didn't even know there was a match between us until after Papa died. He had left a letter outlining his wish for Archibald to look after me. Neither of my parents felt a woman could be alone for long."

"But did you love this man?"

She looked at her hands rather than answer Erin's question. How did she know what love was? Her parents had never let her outside without a chaperone. Archibald was the only man of her age she had ever really spoken to. He was the only one to touch her. Yet when he did, rather than feel loved, she felt dirty. It was odd, but she couldn't relax around him. He didn't feel real, which was rather stupid given he was a nephew of her father's.

"I don't think so, no."

"So where is he now? Is he the reason you were running?"

"I don't know. He said I was confused. He said I was showing signs of mental instability. Maybe it was a family trait. Given I was adopted, how would they know anything about my background? I heard him arguing with the doctor. He suggested I go into an asylum. He told the doctor I was saying odd things. But I never said anything of what he said I said. At least I don't think I did. The days after Mama and Papa died were such a blur. I don't know what I was doing or saying. Maybe he is right."

Erin took her hand. "Shush now. Cathy, I haven't seen any sign of mental illness."

"I thought Mary would know, she being older. I

can't really remember our parents that well. I wanted Archibald to take me to meet her but he got very angry. He accused me of wanting him to mix with riff-raff. We had a big row and he…"

"He what?"

"He said I was insane. He grabbed me and locked me in my room. Told the servants not to come to see me. He slashed his hand and told them I did it. But I swear I didn't. I have never hit anyone in my life."

"How did you get away?"

"Mama's maid helped me. Her name is Jane. She and Toby, he was the groom. Together, they got me out of the house and onto a train to Clover Springs. I don't know why they helped me. Archibald sacked all the other servants. Said they were lazy and corrupt. They'd been stealing from my parents for years. But I don't think they were. They seemed very nice. Toby had been sacked already but he came back when Archibald was away. I think he is Jane's beau. The only reason Archibald kept Jane was because I couldn't cope without her."

CHAPTER 16

"Doc Erin, we got trouble."

"Good morning to you, too, Little Beaver," Doc said smiling at their Indian deputy sheriff. "What kind of trouble?"

"Big kind. I think I got to arrest the woman in your office."

"Cathy? Why? I can't imagine that frail woman doing anything wrong."

"Says here she's wanted for questioning over the death of her parents, theft and fraud."

Erin had to sit down. She didn't know her patient well but she wasn't in a fit state to be capable of anything like that. Unless she had taken opium to dull the guilt.

"I need to put her in the jailhouse, Doc. The Pinkertons are coming for her. Says here they will be here within the week."

"Little Beaver, do you have to? She's ill."

"Sheriff won't like it, Doc. With him in Leadville, it's only me here."

"Leave the sheriff to me. What if I guarantee she will never be left alone? Would that help?"

Little Beaver's smile nearly dazzled her. "Sure will, Doc. I hated the thought of putting Davy Sullivan's sister-in-law in prison. Him and Mary, they have always been good to me and my family."

"I promise there is more to this. That woman in there was starving to death. She doesn't fit the picture of a thief, never mind a fraudster or a murderer."

"Well, you know better than most some people are good at hiding things."

That was true. Look at how well her first husband had deceived her. Little Beaver walked away, but Erin called after him

"Wait, who was she supposed to have killed?"

"Her parents. They were killed in a boat accident on the Hudson River."

"Mr. Prentice, Alicia's friend, may know about these people if they were wealthy. I need to send a telegram.

"Don't you tell nobody that the woman isn't in the jailhouse. I don't want Sheriff getting upset."

"I won't. Thanks, Little Beaver"

The man walked away, waving off her thanks with a wave of his hand. He had such a big heart—if only those who hated him could see past his race and his color.

Erin called Emer and Mrs. Grey outside and explained what had happened, and that from now on Cathy couldn't be left alone.

"Are you going to tell her?"

"Not yet, Mrs. Grey. I don't think she is well enough to handle another shock."

"What about Mary?"

"Yes, I will tell her."

"I would bet money on it that there is more to this story. Cathy a fraudster? She is barely well enough to carry herself, never mind commit fraud. I don't believe a word of it."

"Unfortunately, Emer, it appears some people do or else the Pinkertons wouldn't be on their way. Now, I best get to the telegraph office. See you later."

Erin walked along the street to Martha's house. She had to tell Mary first and then go to the telegraph office. Clover Springs was a small town and news like this had a way of spreading fast.

As luck would have it, Davy was at his ma's house, too.

"Davy, nice to see you. Did you get those issues with your herd sorted out?"

"Not sure yet, Doc. Think we may have some cattle rustlers again. Will know more tomorrow or the next day. I just came into town to see how the missus was doing."

"Don't leave just yet, Davy. I have more news."

"Bad?"

Erin didn't get a chance to answer as Mary came forward, white as a newly washed sheet. "Cathy?"

"Is fine for the moment. Mary, it seems there was some trouble in New York. The Pinkertons are on their way to bring Cathy back home."

"Why?"

"She is wanted for questioning over the death of her adoptive parents. There are also some allegations about theft and fraud."

"Oh, my God, Cathy can't go back there. Davy, we have to take her out to the ranch. We can guard her better."

"That's not possible, Mary. She has to stay at the clinic."

"But why? I can nurse her at home."

"It's that or the jailhouse. Mary, they think Cathy may have involved in her parents' death," Erin said, as gently as she could.

Davy caught his wife just as she fainted. Doc Erin helped her to recover.

"Sorry Doc, I just keep getting dizzy. You can't be serious."

"I am. She is accused of theft and fraud, and also wanted for questioning over the deaths. She hasn't been arrested for murder or else the Law would have demanded her return to New York."

"But she wouldn't need to steal anything. She has enough money to buy Clover Springs, or at least that is the impression we had. Her parents were very wealthy," Mary said, confusion dulling her tone.

"I have some friends in New York. I am going to telegram them and see what I can find out. In the meantime, I want you to come into the office for an examination. I don't like hearing people are dizzy for no good reason."

Mary colored and looked to Davy, who stared back at her, concern for his wife all over his face.

"I don't need an exam, Doc. I haven't said anything yet because I wasn't sure. I am going to have a baby."

Davy's expression was priceless. He threw his hat

in the air and kissed his wife. Then he seemed to remember the reason for Erin's visit and flushed red. "Sorry, for a second I forgot."

"Don't be sorry, Davy. It's nice to get some good news. Now, Mary, I still want to do an exam and you must try to rest. Try not to get upset." At the look on Mary's face, she hastened to add, "At least try, okay."

She left the house to go send her telegrams. She had to see if Mr. Prentice knew anything that may help her friends.

Later she called back to see Cathy. The younger girl was wide awake and looked much better. Mary and Katie happened to call just after Erin arrived back.

"Can we see her please? I can't stand the thought of her being here and not giving her a cuddle."

"I will ask her. Just wait here, Mary."

Mary nodded as Erin went into Cathy's room.

* * *

CATHY LOOKED up as Erin walked into the room.

"Erin, Mrs. Grey was just telling me about Katie's children, they sound adorable."

"They are although at times they drive their ma mad. How are you feeling?"

"Better thank you. Was that Mary I heard you talking to?" Cathy didn't want to get her hopes up but she thought she recognized her sister's voice.

"She wants to speak with you. Can I bring her in?"

Cathy nodded, suddenly losing the ability to speak. Mrs. Grey held her hand and she was glad of the comfort. She looked at the door. It seemed to take forever for Mary to come in. When she did, Katie was with her. Erin brought up the rear.

"Mary, I am so sorry."

"Cathy love, I can't believe it. My prayers have been answered. You are here. I have to pinch myself to believe it is actually you. How are you feeling? When will you be allowed go home? Of course you are staying with Davy and me. We have a big enough house and..."

"Mary for the love of God will you give her a chance to speak," Mrs Grey admonished Mary.

Everyone laughed as Mary blushed. Cathy hugged her closer. "You haven't changed a bit. You always could talk the hind leg off of a donkey."

"Sorry, I know I talk too much. I cry too much too but I am so happy to see you. You can't imagine how much. I love you Cathy."

"I love you too, Mary." Cathy's voice shook with

unshed tears. She looked around the room and found everyone was crying or wiping away tears. Even Mrs. Grey.

"We have missed out on so many years but I promise as soon as you are better, we will make up for them," Mary said between sobs.

Cathy couldn't stop the look of panic on her face, she tried her best but making plans for the future just sounded too daunting.

"Mary, I'm in trouble. Doc Erin is trying to help me but we can't get our hopes up. I may have to go back to New York." Cathy didn't want to admit to her sister she had taken drugs and may be insane. She couldn't exactly just drop the fact Archibald had threatened to put her in an asylum into the first conversation they had in nearly ten years.

"Never. I won't let anyone take you away again, I promise."

Cathy sent Erin a silent plea for help. The doctor stood up.

"Now everyone, let's give Cathy some space. She needs her sleep. Mary, you will have plenty of time to chat again tomorrow and all the days after that. But for now, we need to leave."

Mary looked reluctant but Cathy gave her hand a

squeeze. "I am rather tired Sis, I promise I will be up for more chatting tomorrow. I love you."

"Love you too, Cathy. Can I give you a cuddle?"

Before she could answer, Mary had her arms wrapped around her. A feeling of calm came over her whole body. She was home. Finally!

CHAPTER 17

She sat up in bed, wondering what all the whispering was about. Doc Erin and Emer had been huddled together for a while.

"What's going on?"

"Oh, you're awake. How are you feeling?"

"Like you are hiding something from me. Please tell me. I get very anxious." That was an understatement, but she thought they would understand.

"Cathy, why did you leave New York?"

"I wanted to see Mary."

"But why now?"

Her stomach churned. She had to admit the truth. It was time.

"I was scared Archibald would put me in an asylum. He kept saying I was mad and I did horrible things. But I didn't, I swear. I think he was poisoning me."

"Did you hurt anyone else?"

Shocked, she swiveled to face Emer. "No. Like who?"

"Cathy, we've been told there are some Pinkerton agents on their way to talk to you."

"Archibald must have sent them. But why?"

"I don't know, but it seems there are some questions over your parents' death."

"The accident?" She stared into Erin's eyes. "You mean it wasn't an accident. They were killed on purpose? No, that can't be true. Nobody would do that to them. They didn't have any enemies."

"You can't know that. From what you have told us, your parents were very protective of you."

"Yes, they were, but still. Murder? No, that's wrong. If I was accused of murder why wait until now? The accident was six months ago."

"That's very true. Why aren't they sending the police? It seems very strange," Erin said, thinking aloud.

"Can Archibald order me back to New York? He's my guardian now."

"It would appear so," Erin said, taking Cathy's in hers as the young girl paled. "Don't fret, we will find out what is going on. You just concentrate on getting better."

* * *

"Doc, I found these. I thought Cathy's story sounded familiar. Lawrence keeps all the old newspapers. My husband drives me mad but I guess now they have come in handy I will have to keep my mouth shut."

Doc looked at what Emer was holding. The New York paper with the headline – Couple Killed in Boating Incident.

"That's about Cathy's parents," Mary piped up. They were all sitting in Erin's lounge. Mrs. Grey was watching Cathy, who was still sleeping a lot. Erin was sitting with Michelle on her lap. She'd missed her little girl. Nora was out exploring Clover Springs with Robbie.

"Yes, it is. It says she was thrown clear and hints it may not have been the miracle it first appeared. It doesn't name her as a suspect, though. Seems this Archibald Johnston is a nephew of her adoptive father's. He was made her guardian and is responsible for her unless she marries. He has been quoted as saying it was all very convenient how Cathy escaped but he doesn't actually accuse her of murder."

"Archibald, he's the man who gave her the drugs. At least that's what Cathy says," Erin clarified.

"We have no reason not to believe her. Oh, the poor girl."

"The best protection we have is for Cathy to get married," Erin said bluntly. "Then Archibald cannot put her in an asylum as he is no longer her guardian."

"Doesn't she need his permission to get married?"

"I don't know but we could try it and see. There is more to this story than we know. I can feel it," Erin replied.

"Get married? She's only just arrived in Clover Springs," Mary exclaimed.

"It's not much different from you and I all those years ago. She could marry Abe O'Malley. He seems like a nice, caring young man," Katie said.

"But we don't know him," Mary protested

"Mick does. Says he is a fine man and came from a good family. He is a very talented carpenter, too. Does amazing work with his hands. Paul Kelley was just saying he is going to need help with the building work Robbie needs doing on the new hotel. Then there is the restaurant to build."

"Would Abe do it?" Mary asked.

Abe walked into the room, causing the ladies to gasp.

"Would I do what? Beg your pardon and everything, but you seem to be discussing me. So I guess I should be here."

"Sorry, Abe, didn't mean to but your name happened to come up." Erin turned to the other ladies. "Abe moved in here and let Robbie stay over the saloon. We didn't think Father Molloy would like Nora and Robbie to live under the same roof."

"That was a good idea. Nice to meet you properly, Abe. Never got a chance to thank you for the day you carried Cathy to the clinic," Katie added.

Abe just nodded, the curiosity in his eyes reminding Erin they had been discussing his marriage.

"My sister is in trouble and you could help her. Would you?" Mary asked.

"I would do anything I could, Miss Mary, but I am not sure…" Abe answered.

"That's settled, then. I will ask Father Molloy to arrange the wedding," Mary replied

"Wedding. Now, hold on a minute. I never said anything about getting wed." Abe's panic was evident from his tone.

"But you said you would do anything to help," Mary insisted.

"But that's just a figure of speech. I can't marry

your sister. I ain't never getting married again," Abe confirmed.

"Please, Abe. I know you don't know each other but you are both fine people. She needs protecting. For reasons we don't completely understand, her life may be at risk. Her freedom is certainly in question," Erin tried to explain.

"Can't her rich family help her?" he asked.

"We think they may be part of the problem." Erin was about to explain, but the look on his face stopped her.

CHAPTER 18

Abe looked around the room as everyone stared back at him. Feeling the weight of their expectations, he was about to say no.

"Marry Cathy, stay here in Clover Springs. You will never be out of work again. I married Davy when I didn't know him and we are very happy. As are many of our mail order couples," Mary coaxed.

"I never ordered a mail order bride," he protested.

"Hold on, everyone. It's not right to push Abe into doing this. There must be someone else available," Erin intervened.

"Charlie Staunton wants a wife," Emer added.

"Anyone but him," Erin replied, sending the nurse a look.

Abe didn't know who this Charlie Staunton was but judging by the looks on the ladies faces, he wasn't an option.

"There's a couple of the ranch hands on my place but they are a bit rough around the edges. I am not sure my sister is up to dealing with them, given what she is used to." Mary said, turning her eyes on Abe. She was begging him. He edged away.

"Exactly. Your sister is used to gentlemen, and rich ones at that. I only have the clothes I stand up in."

"You have far more than that. You have a full time job if you want it, a God given talent, old friends and plenty of new ones should you agree to stay." Mary insisted.

"What do you mean when you say her freedom is at risk?" he asked.

"There have been some concerns raised over her parents' accident. It appears that some family members think Cathy may have been responsible."

"I can't marry someone on the wrong side of the law."

"But Abe, that's the weird thing. The law hasn't gotten involved. Not yet, anyway. It's all speculation and rumor. Little Beaver was told the Pinkertons were on their way but why send detectives when there is no mystery? If Cathy was involved, why not just arrest her? Why dope her with drugs or threaten her with an asylum?"

"Who did that?" Abe asked, horrified someone would try to harm a defenseless young girl. Someone like his Pa would do it.

"We believe it was her adoptive father's nephew. He told Cathy her father wanted them to get married. It was news to Cathy. He is also her guardian."

"So he has complete control over her unless she is married to someone else?"

"Yes. We believe as she is over eighteen the marriage would be legal here, but whether that was the case in New York, we don't know."

"But she lives here. And if it stops that man from hurting her, I guess I should marry her. Only if you are sure there is nobody else suitable."

The women shook their heads. All seemed to be in agreement that there was only one candidate – him.

Oh, what the heck. He'd agree to marry her only to keep her safe. It wasn't a lot to ask and people had done things for him before. It was time to return the favor.

"Okay. I'll do it."

* * *

THE WEDDING WAS ARRANGED for the following day. They had to hurry as Cathy had to be married before her guardian arrived with the Pinkertons. Father Molloy conducted the ceremony.

"Cathy, you look beautiful. Try to smile. Abe O'Malley is a nice man," Mary said, hugging her sister. "I know it's all happening very quickly. We haven't even sat down together for a chat but we must protect you. Abe can do that."

"But I don't know him."

"No, but I didn't know Davy and look how happy we are. Abe is caring and smart. He is very talented, too. You will have a good life together.

"Mary, I don't know anything about how to be a wife. I have never made a bed. I don't cook, clean or do any of the stuff a wife is supposed to do."

"I'll help you with that stuff. Abe knows where you came from. He will be patient.

"And what about the other stuff. You know..." Cathy didn't know where to look. She hoped her sister would pick up on what she was trying to say without her having to spell it out. Mama had told her she would tell her everything she needed to know before she got married. But Mama died and she hadn't a clue about how you got pregnant or had a baby or anything.

Mary colored slightly, a pink blush on her cheeks. "Give it time and that will be just fine, too."

Cathy wasn't sure what would be fine, but her sister wasn't about to elaborate. She smoothed down the sides of the dress again. If she didn't go ahead, Archibald would insist she accompany him back to New York. This time he would put her in the asylum just as he threatened if she wasn't hanged for murder first. Her only chance was getting married and having the protection of a husband. That would at least save her from Archibald.

She walked up the aisle her arm on Davy Sullivan's arm. He seemed like a nice man, everything about him agreeing with what Mary had said in her letters. She didn't know him very well but he had agreed to give her away. She saw Abe standing at the altar but he seemed a million miles away. She smiled at him but he didn't seem to notice. Heart hammering, she thanked Davy and turned to the stranger who would become her husband.

* * *

Abe stood in the church with Mick at his side. Despite Mick's chatter about different members of the

Clover Springs community, Abe's mind focused on his last wedding. They hadn't been madly in love but had known each other since they were children. He'd grown up with Sally and everyone assumed they'd get married. They'd been happy together and thrilled when their baby girl had been born. But then the pox came and everything changed. He had made vows to his wife and here less than a year after her death, he was about to marry someone else. How could he do this to her memory now? Marrying a stranger. She'd understand he was doing it to protect the girl. He smiled despite himself. Sally wouldn't have cared about the reasons. She'd been jealous of any girl he'd spent time with, even his baby sister Cara. Now wasn't the time to be thinking ill of his dead wife.

He glanced quickly at his bride. She looked pretty, but most brides looked beautiful on their wedding day. She wasn't the best looking woman he had seen. She looked so scared, her hands were shaking. He took her hand in his in a bid to reassure her all would be okay and she jumped a mile. He released it quickly.

Father Molloy said the service. The words just rattled over his head.

"You may now kiss the bride.

Abe leant over and dropped a kiss on his bride's

cheek. Her skin was so soft. She smelled good, too, a hint of lavender mixing with her natural scent. His body reacted to her presence although his mind told him she was off limits.

CHAPTER 19

The celebration meal after the wedding was an unusual affair. The ladies had out-done themselves. The food on display looked delicious but he couldn't eat a morsel. His new bride obviously felt the same way as she didn't eat anything, either. She kept jumping as if terrified something would happen.

"Cathy, would you like to take a walk for a few minutes. I'd like to talk with you."

He wished she didn't look so scared. He wasn't going to hurt her. He offered her his arm, feeling her shake as she took it. He led her outside, away from the crowd, and walked a little bit. When he knew they were out of earshot, he stopped.

"Cathy, we haven't had a chance to talk much. I just

wanted you to know I won't ever raise a hand to ya. I don't hold with hitting women."

Her eyes opened wider, if that was at all possible. He couldn't help noticing their unusual color. He'd thought they were green but now in the starlight, they looked blue like the river.

"Cathy, can you try not to be so scared?"

"I'm sorry. I…it's just I…well, I never had a husband before."

Was that why she was scared? She thought he was going to demand his rights?

He drew her closer to put his arm around her to help ward off the cold. She looked up at him, reminding him of a doe he once tried to shoot. His pa had whipped him for not pulling the trigger, but he couldn't kill such a beautiful creature. Not when she was staring at him.

He coughed, dispelling the memory. He put a finger under her chin, forcing her to look into his eyes.

"Cathy, I swear I will never force you to do anything. Our marriage is in name only. Doc Erin asked me to protect you and that is what I aim to do."

Was it his imagination or was that a flicker of disappointment in her eyes? It was gone as quick as it came.

He kissed her lightly on the tip of her nose. "Come on, wife, let's go back inside and at least pretend we are happy."

Cathy moved her head and took his arm, but not before he saw the sadness in her eyes once more. He wished more than anything he could get rid of it.

* * *

"Abe, I think its best if you and Cathy came to stay on the ranch. My-sister-in law is rather anxious."

That was the understatement of the century, Abe thought, but he didn't voice his opinion.

"What about Gary? He's been good to me and I promised to help him with the new house." Abe didn't want to seem ungrateful. Hopefully using Gary as an excuse would help his brother-in-law not to take offense.

"I've asked a few of my men to help him. I think it's best if you and Cathy were to move out of town. Away from everyone, but particularly those who cannot keep their noses out of other people's business." Abe followed Davy's gaze to Charlie Staunton and Mrs. Shaw. They seemed to be enjoying themselves, although who had invited them was anyone's guess.

That group was certainly not part of Mick and Erin's crowd.

"Not only would it give you two a chance to get to know one another, but also my wife and her sister will have time together. It means a lot to both of them."

Abe nodded. Who was he to say no to one of the wealthiest men in town?

"I heard you are a skilled carpenter. Paul Kelley is a master of woodcraft. He is married to one of the teachers you met, Laura. They live out on the ranch. Paul would be happy for you to work with him. He has too much work at the moment and with the new hotel and restaurant coming, that's not likely to change."

"I don't need charity, Mr. Sullivan. I pay my own way."

"I know that, Abe, and can you call me Davy. I still look for my pa when anyone addresses me as Mr. O'Sullivan, God rest his soul. We are family now."

Abe shook the man's hand. Family? That was rich. He'd only met Davy a few times but he probably knew him better than he did his wife. What had he done?

"Cookie is looking forward to having you around, too. Says he wants to catch up with all that is happening in Noelle."

Abe nodded. Cookie had gotten back from Noelle a day or so ago. He hadn't had time to catch up with his friend. "Where will we live? I'd rather not share your house, too."

Davy laughed before hitting him hard on the back. "To be honest, that makes me happy. The idea of living with family isn't appealing to me, either. There's a small house on the ranch. Paul, Laura and a couple of the men are tidying it up right now, getting it ready for when you come out."

"You knew I'd say yes." Abe wasn't sure he liked that.

"We were hoping you'd say yes. Little Beaver lives nearby so he can reassure the sheriff Cathy won't run away."

"Cathy won't go anywhere. She has to prove her innocence first." Abe couldn't help but voice his protectiveness of Cathy.

CHAPTER 20

Cathy pinched herself – she must be dreaming. Here she was married to a man she barely knew, surrounded by people most of whom she had never met. She closed her eyes, missing her Mama and Papa. Mama had spoken so many times about what her wedding would be like. She would host it at a Fifth Avenue Hotel and the guest list would read like a who's who of New York. There would be champagne and caviar, her dress would be made in Paris from the finest of silks and satins. Papa would buy her a beautiful house near the beach, but most of the time they would live in a mansion near her parents.

"Cathy, are you all right? You are a bit pale."

"I am fine. Thank you, Doc."

"It's a lot to take in. I came from New York almost two years ago. It is very different here but give these people a chance. The majority of them are kind and considerate and will do their best to help you."

"Mrs. Shaw and Mrs. Kelley have already paid their respects." Cathy stopped speaking at the look of distaste on the doctor's face.

"Keep well away from those troublemakers. They may appear like innocent ladies but neither adjective is appropriate for that pair."

Cathy didn't argue. They'd seemed nice to her, but then she was hardly a good judge of character. She had trusted Archibald completely. But Papa had, too. Papa always said you could trust blood more than anything. But then he'd forgotten Archibald wasn't her real cousin. Papa always forgot Cathy was adopted. He treated her like a real daughter. *He should have been here to walk me down the aisle.* She brushed away a tear. If Papa was here she wouldn't be in Clover Springs.

"Cathy, would you like to go now? Seems your sister and her husband have arranged a new home for us."

"For us, you mean just the two of us?"

"Yes. A house on their ranch. It means you get to see Mary and her children every day. And Ben. He seems to like you."

Was her new husband teasing her? She looked into his eyes. They seemed to be smiling at her. She wished she knew him better. Was he always this kind or was this his people face? Would he turn into a monster behind closed doors?

"Are you ready?"

As ready as she would ever be. She took his hand and held on tight as he said goodbye on their behalf.

"Wait. You forgot to throw the bouquet. That's tradition."

Cathy clutched the flowers in her spare hand. She let the group of ladies gather together before pitching them over her head. The crowd started laughing. She turned quickly to make sure she hadn't hit anyone. Mrs. Grey was holding the flowers, her face a picture of embarrassment.

"Sorry, I didn't mean…" Cathy started to apologize, but her apology was cut off by the teasing going on around her.

"Poor Mrs. Grey, she is never going to live this down. Come on, Mrs. O'Malley. Let's go home."

Cathy blinked at her new name before picking up her skirt in one hand and holding her husband's hand as she walked to the wagon. Instead of helping her in, he lifted her as if she weighed nothing at all. He held her closer than she believed necessary, but it was pleasant. He smelled of ferns and something woody. Her pulse beat faster as his breath caught the side of her ear. It was almost as if he kissed her lightly but she must have imagined it. He tucked a rug around her before going around to the other side of the wagon and climbing in.

"Are we waiting for the others?"

"Cookie rode ahead to start the fire, but I think we will leave the others to the party. I don't really want them coming to our new house with us. I'd rather do that as just the two of us. Do you mind?"

Cathy shook her head. She didn't mind, not really. In fact, she was kind of excited. Her new husband was proving to be kind and thoughtful. Maybe this marriage could work out for real.

* * *

COOKIE WAS WAITING for them as the wagon pulled into the ranch. He congratulated Cathy and gave Abe a big hug. Then he said he'd mind the wagon and pointed them in the direction of a small wooden house with smoke billowing out of the chimney.

"Lit the fire to keep you warm. Mrs. Higgins dropped over a basket of food to save you cooking tonight. Nice to meet ya, Mrs. O'Malley. See you in the morning."

And he was gone, leaving Cathy and Abe standing outside their new home. Abe opened the door and Cathy was about to walk through when he surprised her by picking her up.

"Can't have you walking into your new home. It's traditional for the man to carry his bride over the threshold."

Cathy buried her face in his neck, her soft skin feeling nice against his. She smelled so good, her soft warm body next to his was playing havoc with his thoughts. He let her down rather abruptly, hoping she wouldn't notice his reaction to her nearness. Her eyes opened wider as she looked around.

"Looks right nice, doesn't it?" He said.

"But it's so small? Where is the bathroom and the bedrooms?"

He looked at his bride, wondering what she had expected. This wasn't New York.

"The necessary is out the back, I guess. I should go and look. The bedroom will be through that door, I imagine."

He pointed at a door before leaving to explore the outside.

* * *

CATHY TOOK off her hat and placed it on the table. She opened the door which led into a large bedroom, dominated by a big double bed. Her bag was sitting on the bed with her nightdress laid out on one pillow. She blushed. Mary must have set things up for her or else it was their housekeeper, Mrs. Higgins. She looked around the room. The quilted cover matched the curtains, making it look very cozy. There was a small dresser, on top of which was one picture frame. She picked it up to see a picture of her sister's wedding day. Mary looked just as nervous as she had today. There was a note under it.

That day was the start of something special. Allow yourself to find happiness. Mary x

SHE FOLDED the note up and put it in her pocket. Not that she didn't want Abe to read it, but she didn't want to put pressure on him. She knew he had married her to protect her from Archibald. He could no longer decide whether she ended up in an asylum—although she wasn't sure how the marriage would protect her from the law.

CHAPTER 21

Abe came in, bringing the cold with him. He shut the door behind him just as she came out of the bedroom. There was only one. Where was he going to sleep? He didn't expect them to share the same bed, did he? She couldn't meet his eyes.

"The necessary is out the back a little way. I can show you if you like. Before you get undressed. Its cold out there."

Embarrassed like she had never been before, Cathy nodded. She followed him to the outhouse.

"You can go back inside now. I will be fine."

"If you're sure?"

She was certain she didn't want him standing outside and waiting for her. She would rather face a grizzly bear than that. Did they have grizzlies out here? Oh, why had she agreed to this wedding?

"Cathy?"

"Please. I will be fine."

He walked back to the house. She ran after him just as soon as she was finished, not wanting to be outside alone. She washed her hands at the sink as he started to unpack the basket Mrs. Higgins had left.

"I stayed in the bunkhouse with Cookie when I first got here. Mrs. Higgins is a wonderful cook. Are you hungry?"

She was. The smells coming from the basket made her stomach growl.

"Sure sounds like you are."

"Abe!"

"What?"

"A gentleman wouldn't comment."

Abe looked at her, smiling. "I guess there's lots of things you need to teach me. I ain't used to acting like a gentleman."

Yet, he was. He had opened the door for her, offered to wait for her, carried her into the house. He acted like the perfect gentleman. Well, apart from commenting on her growling stomach but that was loud enough for them to hear up in the big house.

She sat at the table as he dished out two plates.

"Do you want coffee or tea with that?"

"No, thank you."

"Milk?"

He poured each of them a cup of milk, causing her to giggle.

"What? Did I not pour it in a gentlemanly fashion?"

"I was just wondering how many people drank milk on their wedding day?"

Abe looked at the cup and then back at her. "Guess you should have been drinking champagne or something?"

She kicked herself. He seemed a little hurt. "I would rather have milk. Champagne bubbles make me sneeze and mama always said that wasn't ladylike."

He grinned at her and in that second, she had an image of what he must have looked like as a little boy growing up.

Embarrassed to be staring at him, she looked down at her plate.

"You need to eat a lot. You are way too skinny."

"Pardon?"

"Oh, Lord, Cathy I can't help it. I was brought up to say what's on my mind. I wasn't meaning you don't have a fine figure. You do, but you just need a little fattening up."

"You make me sound like a turkey coming up to Thanksgiving."

"That's not what I meant...wait, you're teasing me, aren't you?"

She smiled. He had a way of making her want to smile all the time. "Just a little."

He laughed, making her laugh, too.

She struggled to cut some of the meat. He leaned over, took her plate and cut it up into little strips. Then rather than hand her the plate back, he fed her. It felt wicked to be eating from his fingers but good at the same time. The food was delicious, but it could have tasted like wood chippings for all she cared. She was caught up in the mood. The firelight flickered as he leaned in. She thought he was going to kiss her. She wanted him to, but he wiped her face.

"You got juice on your chin."

Mortified, she grabbed the napkin and wiped her face and hands clean. Then she stood and began to clear the dishes.

"Leave those until the morning. Come over here."

She let him take her by the hand and lead her over to the fire. There was only one chair. Were they supposed to share it? Rather than sit on the chair, he motioned for them both to sit on what looked like a bearskin in front of the fire. It was soft and furry to touch. He sat first and then drew her to his side, his weight supporting hers.

"Tell me something about yourself, Cathy."

She didn't know where to start.

"Do you remember Ireland?" he prompted.

She closed her eyes, leaning back against him, and told him the earliest memories she had of Ireland. She was running through a field of daffodils, chasing after Mary who was ahead of her. Her mam and da were behind her with other adults. It must have been some sort of feast day or festival, because there were lots of adults. They were happy, too, not sad like when they had to leave.

He was a good listener. He didn't interrupt, but he was playing with her hair the whole time. It made her feel funny inside. She found herself telling him other stories. Nothing sad. She didn't want to think about leaving Mary behind at the orphanage or her parents drowning. She told him stories of being sent to private schools, where the girls made fun of her accent. Her parents had moved her to another school when they found out.

"It was like I was made of glass. They were always trying to protect me. I think it was because their real children died."

"What happened to them? Sickness?"

She had to concentrate now on her words, his caresses were making it hard to think.

"I don't think so. I never knew for certain. It was one thing I wasn't allowed to talk about. Well, two really. They didn't like me talking about Mary or my family. They didn't want to talk about Luke and Christina. They said they died suddenly in some tragic accident. I guess it must have been too painful for them."

"Hmmm."

"Abe, are you listening to me?" She looked around to find him gazing down at her, a funny look in his eyes. He stared at her face and seemed to focus on her lips before traveling back up to her eyes again. He moved his head slowly, as if waiting for her to make the next move. She reacted instinctively and stretched up against him to meet his kiss.

His lips were softer than she'd expected. Although he had shaved that morning, he had stubble already and it tickled her face. She had turned her body so she was lying against him. His arms didn't move, but just held her close. His lips moved away from hers and he kissed her eyes, her nose, her ear and then along her chin back to her mouth. If this was what being married was like, it was wonderful. Her breathing came more rapidly as he continued to kiss her, his kisses getting harder. She wasn't sure what to do but instinctively she knew there was something more. She broke the kiss panting, her eyes glued to his.

"Cathy, I think you should go to bed now."

"Alone?" She flushed bright red as soon as she realized she'd spoken aloud.

"There is only one bed so it is best I sleep out here tonight."

"Don't you like kissing me?"

He smiled and pulled her to him, but instead of kissing her on the mouth, he kissed her head like you would a child.

"Yes, I like kissing you a lot but we have only just met and I think it would be better to get to know each other first before we take the next step."

"Oh." She didn't say anything else. What could she say? He was older and had been married before. She should listen to him. Even if it felt wrong.

"Goodnight."

"Goodnight, Cathy. Sleep well."

CHAPTER 22

Abe listened as his wife moved around the bedroom. He could imagine her changing for bed.

Think about cabbages. He hated cabbage – about the only food he couldn't eat. He hated the smell of it cooking, too. He tried to block out the thoughts of his lovely young wife with thoughts of cabbages, but it didn't work. He decided the fire needed more firewood. Even splitting logs in the cold didn't stop his blood from roaring through his veins. He was trying to be patient and kind, but it sure was hard work.

"What are you up to, son? You have a row with your missus already?

"No, Cookie, I just thought it best to get ahead with some chores."

"Really? Do you think you are going to get snowed in or something?"

Cookie indicated the stack of firewood with the lit end of his cigarette. "Seems to me there is trouble in the new family."

"Leave me be, Cookie."

"I will, lad, but remember I am here if you want to talk. I know you been on your own a long time. Been a man since your pa died, maybe even before that. But that don't mean you don't need a friend. I have a good ear for listening and as you know, I ain't one for much talking."

"Cookie, I appreciate it, I do. It's just difficult."

"Why? You're a man, she's a woman. A pretty one, at that. Many would consider themselves lucky to be married to a gal like that."

"We only just met. She's real innocent. I don't think she's ever been kissed before. Never mind."

"Good for you lad for thinking of her feelings, but don't leave her alone for too long. From what I hear, that little gal in there been through a heck of a lot of trouble. She needs a friend, too."

"You want me to be her friend?"

"Why not? You're her husband. If a man's wife isn't his best friend, then he got marriage problems."

Cookie wandered off, leaving a trail of smoke in his wake.

Abe put down the axe and went back inside. He took up a towel to wipe his face and neck, but stopped at the sound of crying. Cathy was upset.

He knocked on the door before going inside.

"Cathy, what's wrong?"

"Nothing."

"But you are crying."

"No, I'm not."

He was about to leave when he heard another muffled sob. He went over to the bed and brushed the hair from her face. It was hard to see in the moonlight. She hadn't pulled the curtains

"You are. Tell me what's wrong. Maybe I could help."

"I thought you were upset with me," she said, her voice croaky with tears.

He couldn't believe it. He'd been trying to be kind and had only succeeded in upsetting her. He hated women crying. It reminded him all too painfully of his childhood. He smoothed back her silky hair from her face. "Whatever made you think that?"

"You kissed me and sent me to bed. Alone."

He gathered her to him, not wanting to explain what she obviously didn't understand.

"Would you prefer I slept here with you?" He felt rather than saw her head nod in answer.

"Okay. Just let me make sure the fire is safe. I will be back in a minute."

Saying his prayers quickly, he prayed for patience and restraint. His bride was upset enough without him doing anything to scare her further.

CHAPTER 23

The next morning, Cathy woke up to the smell of fried bacon. Remembering the night before, she didn't want to get out of bed. She was so embarrassed. She had clung to Abe and more or less demanded he share the bed with her. What must he think of her?

At the knock on the door, he pushed his head around.

"Come on, sleepy head. The day's a wastin'."

"Coming," she mumbled. She threw on her dress as quickly as she could. Pinning her hair up, she went out to find the table set, coffee in the cups and a large plate of food in two spaces.

"Thank you. I should have been up earlier."

"I thought you said you weren't sure how to cook."

"Oh, you heard that? I thought Mary was the only one listening," Cathy spoke to her plate. She didn't like admitting to being useless.

"I always hear when it's important, like keeping my stomach fed. I like cooking. I can show you what you need to know. But for now, just relax."

She wondered what she had done to meet such a kind man. Everything on her plate tasted wonderful. Partly because it was so fresh, but mainly because she knew she could eat it safely. Abe wouldn't drug her.

"You sure worked up an appetite, didn't you, Mrs. O'Malley?"

Cathy stopped eating.

"What? Don't tell me you are one of those women who don't think they should eat a decent meal."

"No. You called me Mrs. O'Malley."

"That's your name now. Don't you like it?"

"I do. It just sounds so strange…but in a good way." She smiled back at him.

"What are your plans for today?"

"I thought I would go and see Mary. She said she would teach me some useful things. Can't see myself sitting playing the piano or doing embroidery all day around here."

"I don't know. Reckon if we moved the bed out to the barn, you could fit a piano in that room."

"Abe! Be serious."

"Yes, dear."

She threw a biscuit at him and it hit him straight on the forehead. He looked so stunned, she wasn't sure if he was annoyed or not, but he just started to laugh. Then she was laughing, too.

Cookie knocked on the door and walked in.

"Morning, folks. Nice to hear laughter this time of the morning. Abe, you ready? We got to go out and see to the fences on the north side today."

"I thought Paul Kelley was going to show me some stuff."

"He is, but he went into town with his missus so unless you want to sit around chatting all day, your only option is to come with me. Course if you gone soft…" Cookie winked at Cathy.

"I will be right with you."

With a quick kiss on her cheek, he shoved another biscuit in his mouth, grabbed his gun and his hat and was gone.

* * *

Cathy didn't get a chance to think about what she would do for the day as Mary arrived on her doorstep carrying her namesake. "It's time you meet Cathy junior. Why don't you come on up to the house and we can talk. Mrs. Higgins has been cooking again. She bakes the most delicious cookies."

"Mary, you haven't changed a bit. You always talked a lot."

"Oh, I think I might be worse now. I cry easily, too. When I was reading your letters, oh my goodness. I think I cried a river of tears. We missed out on so much, Cathy."

"We did, but think about what could have happened. If my parents had adopted you as well, you wouldn't have any of this. Ben would still be stuck in the orphanage."

"That's true, I never thought of that. Who told you the story about Ben? Wasn't my husband so romantic?"

"Katie told me and yes, he was. He really seems to adore you."

"He does. I love him, too. His ma is so nice to me and Katie is now my real sister. Oh, Cathy, I am so happy. But I am nervous ,too. What if something goes wrong?"

Cathy didn't get a chance to point out she could be

heading to New York to face criminal charges. They had arrived at Mary's house. Mrs. Higgins was waiting on the porch and greeted her like she was a long lost member of her family. She held the door open as they walked into Mary's house. It was stunning. It was immediately evident Davy was well off. The whole place was huge.

"You could have moved in here with us. There is plenty of room, but Dave said your husband didn't want to."

"He must have felt it was better for us to share something smaller to get to know each other better." Cathy had no idea why Abe hadn't taken her sister up on the offer, but she felt she had to stand up for him anyway. Being loyal to one's husband was the start of a good marriage. At least that is what she had read in one of her mama's books. She hadn't any idea of how to make a marriage work, really. She couldn't cook her husband nice meals or make him shirts or do any of the other things these women seemed to do.

"I almost forgot. We are going to Katie's for the quilting party next week. Will you come? Sorcha will be there and her sister, Emer – you met her at Doc's. Erin will come if she isn't too busy. Mrs. Grey will be there and plenty of other women from the town. It's a great way to get to know people."

"But Mary, I don't know how to quilt."

"That's okay. I can show you. I am just so excited to have you here."

They sat and chatted all day long, exchanging memories of Ireland and telling each other what had happened during the years they had been apart.

"Did you read my letters?"

"Yes, Cathy, every one. I can't understand your mama not sending them on. But let's forget about the years we missed and concentrate on the good ones ahead."

Cathy wished she could share her sister's optimism, but she couldn't help feeling Archibald hadn't finished with her just yet.

"Oh, Mary, is that the time. Abe will be home and I haven't anything ready for his dinner. Not that I know how to cook but I don't even know if the fire is still lit."

"Don't worry, come here for dinner. Mrs. H always cooks too much. Tomorrow we can start some lessons on how to cook basics, like roasts and stuff."

Cathy agreed to stay, but said she had to check on the fire. She ran back to the house to find Abe sitting in front of the dying embers. He looked as if he was trying to build it up again.

"Sorry, I got chatting with Mary. She's invited us to dinner."

"Please tell me you said no."

Cathy stared at him. Was he angry?

"Sorry, I said yes. What's wrong? Don't you want to go?"

"I thought after all the fuss yesterday we might just be able to enjoy our own company tonight."

She colored. She hadn't thought he might not want to go.

"I thought you might like a proper meal. I still don't know how to cook."

"Cathy, stop trying to be something you ain't. I told ye I would teach you. Just let me get changed before we head back to your sister's."

"Don't you like Mary?" she asked him, biting the side of her nail.

"I think she is a lovely woman. Why would you ask that?"

"You don't seem so keen on going to her house and she said she offered to have us stay there, but you said no."

"I did that so we can get used to one another first before we have to pretend to be a couple. Was I wrong? Maybe you would be more comfortable there."

"No, it's fine. Mary talks a lot."

He smiled at her and her stomach twisted in a funny way. She wanted him to smile all the time.

"She does, but I thought all women did."

She burst out laughing at him teasing her. He grinned back. How much easier he was to be around than her cousin back in New York. She frowned. She didn't want to think about Archibald. Not now.

CHAPTER 24

The days passed and Cathy got herself into a routine of sorts. She had breakfast with Abe—he cooked, she cleaned up. Then after he went to work, she made her way over to Mary's house where Mrs. H was trying to teach her how to cook. The housekeeper had plenty of patience, which was a good thing as Cathy seemed to be totally clueless. As the days went on, she was finding it hard to sleep and her memory seemed to have deserted her completely.

In the evenings she went home with dinner in tow. Mrs. H refused to let Abe cook for himself after a hard day's work. Abe didn't comment after that first evening when he said he didn't mind cooking for them.

After dinner was Cathy's favorite time of the day.

Abe would sit with her in front of the fire and they exchanged stories of how they grew up. They had read some of the same books, so they discussed them. Cathy told him about going to theaters and shows in New York and other cities. Abe told her about his brothers and sisters. He often talked about his ma, too. She sounded like a nice lady. He never mentioned his pa, only to tell her he died when Abe was younger.

Despite being happy, Cathy was agitated. Abe said it was bound to be nerves about what was happening in New York. Nobody had heard anything since. Abe suggested that was a good thing, but Cathy wasn't so sure. She grew snappy and tired. Every night when Abe was asleep, she tossed and turned, unable to relax. She really wanted some of her medicine but she had run out. She didn't want to ask Abe to get her some as she sensed from things he had said, he wouldn't. A couple of times he had upset her and she snapped at him. He had gone to work leaving her feeling guilty as she knew it was her and not him that was in the wrong. She tried to be nicer in the evenings when he got home but somehow she got worse rather than better.

She decided it was because everyone was looking after her and treating her like a child. She was an adult now, a married woman. She wanted to show everyone she could be independent, so decided to ride into town. Ben helped her with the horse.

"She's Miss Mary's horse, Mrs. O'Malley. She is nice and gentle."

"Thank you, Ben, and please call me Cathy."

"Sure thing, Miss Cathy."

She smiled as he added the Miss to her name although for all intents and purposes she was his aunt. Her sister's adoption of Ben was another sign of Mary's care and consideration for others.

She sat straighter. She had to put aside her worries and concentrate on just riding into town. She was a married woman now and it was time everyone believed she wasn't a fragile little girl.

She enjoyed the ride. The signs of nature opening up in anticipation of summer were all around her—baby birds chirping in their nests, their mamas flying around them protectively. The sun shone and although it wasn't very warm, it wasn't cold, either. She didn't break out in a sweat while riding. As she came into town, she nodded to people who greeted her but she didn't see anyone she knew to say hello to. Dismounting, she tied the horse to the rail outside the store.

"Cathy, what are you doing in town? Is Mary with you?"

Despite Katie's smile, her comment annoyed her. Why would Mary be with her. She wasn't her keeper.

"No, just me."

"Oh. Do you have time for tea?"

"No, thank you, Katie. I came to buy some candy for Abe. He has a real sweet tooth. I need to learn how to make cookies and things but in the meantime, store bought candy will suffice."

"Yes, he does. Most men do, in fairness. I know my Daniel finds it hard to resist. Here you go, then. Is there anything else?"

She should really think about some new clothes but she didn't know how to make dresses. She decided to wait a while as she couldn't buy them from the rack. She didn't know how much money she had.

"Mary said she is coming to your quilting party on Thursday. Could I tag along? I've never quilted but I am quite good at embroidery."

"Sure you can come, Cathy. You will get to meet the other ladies in town. Not all of us are good with needles. Just ask Sorcha."

"I haven't seen her yet. I remember her from the orphanage. The nuns were always telling her off for her sewing."

"She hasn't changed much. She will be here on Thursday."

Katie had to serve another customer, so Cathy left. She was walking down the street toward the doctor's office when she bumped into Mrs. Shaw and Mrs. Kelley. Mary had warned her to stay away from Ma Kelley, as she called her. Cathy didn't know why. Paul Kelley, Laura's husband, was very nice and this woman was his mother.

"Good morning, ladies."

"Morning, Mrs. O'Malley. Fine morning isn't it?"

"Yes, Mrs. Shaw."

"Were you on the way to see Doc Erin?"

Taken aback by the woman's nosiness, she just nodded.

"We understand you had problems. It is difficult to lose both parents in the unfortunate circumstances. Easy to see how one could find relief in a bottle."

She stood motionless, almost afraid to breathe. How did these ladies know so much about her? Who had told them?

"Still, it must be a relief to be married now. Although Mr. O'Malley is probably not what your dear parents envisaged for you. Is that why you fell out with them? Were you always a bit wild?"

Before she could answer, Ma Kelley turned to Mrs. Shaw. "Of course we saw that with all those orphan girls who came here as mail order brides. They really lowered the whole tone of our lovely little town. When I think of what my Paul…"

"Paul and Laura seem very happy together, Mrs. Kelley. Now, excuse me. I must be on my way."

She sped off before the ladies could stop her. Picking up her skirts allowed her to walk faster, but in reality she wanted to run. She pushed open the door of the doctor's office, hoping Erin would be there but she wasn't. Mrs. Grey was on duty.

"Good morning, Cathy. How are you today? You seem a bit overwrought?"

"Fine, thank you, or at least I would be if Mrs. Shaw and Mrs. Kelley didn't seem to know all my business. Can you please tell Erin I need to speak to her?"

Mrs. Grey raised her eyebrows at Cathy's tone but Cathy simply looked away.

"Cathy, sit down and I will make you some tea. You can then tell me what our neighborhood gossips had to say. You can't pay them any attention. Those two *ladies* take pleasure in making others miserable."

She didn't respond. She couldn't. She didn't know whether to scream or cry. As she sat there, her eyes were drawn to the room Erin kept her medications in. She looked around her. Mrs. Grey would be a while making the tea. She had hurt her ankle the previous week and was rather slow on her legs. She should really have offered to make the tea rather than let the older woman do it but she hadn't been thinking straight.

Standing up she walked over to the door expecting it was locked but it wasn't. She pushed it open. She knew where the key for the cabinet was. She had spent enough time in the clinic. Taking the key and keeping one ear out for Mrs. Grey, she opened the cabinet and took a brown bottle from it. She locked it again and was sitting back at the outside table when Mrs. Grey returned.

"Sorry for taking so long, dear. I reckon I should listen to Doc and rest my leg. It is cramping more than normal today."

"I am sorry, Mrs. Grey. I should have made the tea. I was just so angry at what those ladies said."

"Honestly, my dear, you shouldn't worry about them. They are two of the loneliest people in town. Poor Paul Kelley doesn't spend a minute more than he has to with his ma. The things that awful woman said about Laura don't bear repeating. She rarely sees her grandchildren, either. Now, how are things going for your out at the ranch."

"Fine, thank you." She lied. How could she tell this woman who seemed to master everything she tried how much of a failure she was? She couldn't boil water, never mind cook anything.

She drank her tea as quickly as she dared, the brown bottle feeling huge against her leg. Taking the tea cups up to the little kitchen, she washed them and then took her leave of Mrs. Grey.

She was eager to get home. She had to walk back to where her horse was tethered and to do that, she had to pass by Mrs. Shaw again. She was talking to a different lady this time, a younger woman. She walked past without a second look, not caring if she seemed rude. She didn't want to speak to that woman again.

"Ma Kelley was telling me all about her earlier. She is a disgrace. Adopted, she was, and how did she repay her parents? By murdering them. How she has the nerve to walk down our streets. Of course, it's only because she is protected by Davy Sullivan. His money has obviously greased a lot of hands."

With tears in her eyes, she mounted her horse and almost knocked over the deputy sheriff in the process.

"Miss Cathy, you cannot listen to people. Empty vessels make most noise."

She didn't respond but looked back at Mrs. Shaw, who was now staring openly at her.

"Good day, Deputy," she mumbled before nudging the horse into a fast trot. She needed to get home.

She didn't notice anything about the trip home, only the fact it seemed to take forever. She was glad to see Ben. He would look after the horse for her.

"Are you all right, Miss Cathy? You look upset?"

"I am fine, thank you, Ben. Would you mind seeing to the horse? I have a headache."

"Of course, Miss Cathy. You look right pale. Do you want me to fetch Ma?"

"No!" she answered sharply causing a look of hurt in his eyes. "Sorry, Ben. I didn't mean to snap. My head is fit to burst."

"Don't you worry none about me. You go lie down. You will feel better later."

"Thank you, Ben. You are such a lovely young man. No wonder Mary is so proud of you."

She walked back to her house, praying she wouldn't see anyone. Abe wasn't home. He'd ridden out early that morning with Cookie and wasn't expected back until later.

She took as much of the medicine as she dared. She hoped it would be enough to send her to sleep. She never wanted to wake up again.

CHAPTER 25

He worked alongside Cookie all day, but his mind was restless. He should speak to Mary about Cathy. Or maybe Doc Erin. There was something wrong with his wife and he wasn't sure what it was. She wasn't happy, of that he was certain, but it seemed to be more than just missing her parents. She was snappy and agitated. He sometimes found her staring into space despite the fact whatever she had tried to cook was overflowing or burning. It was like she wasn't living in reality. Was she mad? She had told him that is what the Archibald guy from New York had told her.

Yet when she was in a more normal frame of mind, she was funny and really interesting to speak to.

"You wool-gathering again, Abe?"

"Sorry, Cookie."

Cookie put down his tools and took out his water bottle. "What's the matter, son? Your head is not on right today. Hasn't been for a few days."

"I...oh, it's nothing."

"Come on, spit it out. Ain't nothing. You can't hit a nail straight. What's going on."

"It's Cathy. She seems different."

"Different how? You two are only getting to know each other. That's going to take time, son."

"Yes, I know but..."

"It ain't going to be like it was with Sally. You two grew up together in the same place. You knew everything there was to know."

"This isn't about where we grew up, Cookie. It's something else. Something she said."

"Come on, lad. Talk to me. I ain't going to tell nobody. Your missus won't know you talked to me."

"I think she might be mad," Abe stared his old friend right in the eyes.

Cookies mouth dropped open.

"I don't mean it mean, like, but she said her cousin said she was. And she sure acts funny at times. Like she scratches her skin a lot to the point it bleeds. And she has shaking fits. And then she..."

"Your missus ever been given drugs?"

"They gave her something when her pa and ma died. Why?"

"Sounds to me like she was given laudanum when her folks died and now she is missing it. Happened to lots of men after the war. Some never gave up their cravings. Others did, but it took time."

"Cravings?" Abe croaked.

"Yeah, bit like your pa. He probably didn't always drink like he did near the end."

"Not till he lost his arm. But then he was always hot-tempered, so it wasn't just the drink."

"Yeah but he got a taste for it and kept drinking," Cookie paused. "Same with that laudanum stuff. I should know. I was a drinker. Lost me my family."

He stared at Cookie, not knowing what to say. He'd never seen him with a drink in his hand but hadn't questioned it.

"Why don't you go home and see your missus. Try talking to her a little. She's been through a lot in her short life."

"I guess." He didn't want to have to deal with addiction again. It had been bad enough with his pa. But Cathy was his wife now, his responsibility.

"Abe, if anyone can help that young lady, you can. You got a big heart. She is a nice girl, too. She just needs a chance."

He nodded in response to Cookies advice, although what he wanted to do was scream. He had enough issues of his own without taking on someone else's. Why had he called in to see Mick and Cookie? He should have kept on riding. Now he had someone else depending on him. What if she left him, too?

He walked slowly back to the house he shared with his wife, Diamond walking along beside him, nudging his shoulder as if she wanted to try to comfort him. Lord, he was going mad. What was he doing getting ideas about a horse?

He put Diamond in the barn meeting Ben on the way.

"Your missus seemed to have a rough time in town today."

"Cathy was in town? Why? With who?"

"I don't know. I didn't ask but she seemed upset."

"Can you take care of Diamond for me ,Ben? I will go check on her."

"Sure. I wanted to call Ma but Cathy nearly bit my head off. Figured it was better to leave her alone."

Abe didn't respond. Cathy had bit his head off more than once, so he could understand the boy's reluctance.

He pushed the door of the house open, calling her name but there was no response. Nothing was cooking and the house was quiet. He pushed open the bedroom door. There was a funny smell in the room, not one he recognized. It was bitter, though. He hoped it wasn't a perfume she liked. He moved closer to the bed. She was fast asleep. She looked so peaceful. He was stupid to be thinking anything else, she was just tired. Then he spotted the bottle.

CHAPTER 26

"Cathy. Oh, dear God, no. Not again. Cathy?" He pulled her into his arms, shaking her but her head just lolled to the side. He lay her back down and, putting his head to her chest, he could make out a faint heart beat. She was alive. But she had to wake up. Picking her up, he took her outside to the horse trough. It was all he could think of. He dunked her in it fully clothed while yelling for Ben to go for his ma.

Cathy didn't react to the water at first so he dunked her again. Then she woke up spluttering and coughing. He gave her a drink, forcing her to drink more of it than she wanted, as he hoped she vomited again and again. That had to be a good thing, to get the poison from her system. All the time he was yelling her name. "Cathy, don't you dare leave me. Do you hear me?"

Screaming loudly, Mary came running closely followed by a number of other people. He ignored them and kept dunking Cathy's head and making her vomit.

"What on earth. Stop it, stop hurting her," Mary screamed.

"I ain't hurting her. She hurt herself. We need Doc Erin. Send someone quick."

"You take her. It will be faster," Mary responded.

"I got your horse ready," Ben said.

"No. Stop." At Cookie's shout, everyone stopped. Cookie walked over to him and spoke quietly.

"Get her back into your house now, lad. Strip her out of those wet clothes and get her to bed."

"Mary heat up some water –enough for a number of baths." Cookie didn't check if anyone was listening but kept giving orders. "Ben, mount up and go for Doc Erin. Tell her it's an emergency. The rest of you go home and if you are the praying type start praying. Even if you aren't, start praying."

Abe lifted his unconscious wife in his arms and took her back to the house. He was about to put her on the bed when Cookie stopped him.

"No good putting her on the bed, you will only wet

the sheets. You got to strip her and get her into the bed before she catches a chill."

"Cookie, she took that stuff. I don't know how much. But how could she?"

"She wasn't thinking straight, lad. I guess she just wanted to sleep. That's all. Don't let your mind think anything else."

He couldn't move, but stood there with her lying against his chest. Her pulse seemed weaker.

"Come on, lad. Get her undressed. I will make coffee and heat up this place. Move, Abe. Now."

Abe started to undress her. Cathy would be mortified, but who else could do it? She was his wife, if in name only. She was even thinner than he had first imagined. She looked so small in the bed, so fragile. He stripped off his wet clothes and changed into something dry. He then put her into a nightdress, feeling she would prefer to have her modesty.

He held her close, trying to warm her up with his body. Had he done the right thing in making her come around and vomit? Doc Deane used to say it was a good think for a drunk to vomit as it took some of the poisons away, but did that work for this stuff, too. How had she got it? Who would be stupid enough to give a woman of her age a full bottle?

Cookie knocked at the door. "Try to wake her up,

lad. We will give her some coffee. Easy, though. You don't want to burn her."

"Did I do the right thing?"

"In waking her? Yes, absolutely. She has to fight this now. But maybe with you at her side, she'll see she has friends."

"Cookie, you've seen this before, haven't you?"

"Yes, son. Too many times to count. The effects of the war lasted longer than the fighting."

"Did everyone recover?"

Cookie didn't answer. His silence spoke volumes.

CHAPTER 27

She was so cold. Shivering so much her teeth rattled. Her head ached and she was desperate for more of the medicine. It would help her —it always did. She opened her eyes, shutting them tight again as the light hurt them. What was he doing here? He should be at work. She squinted at him.

"Cathy, wake up. Please open your eyes."

She opened them, although not fully as it hurt too much. He was worried about her. She could tell from the tone of his voice, but why? She was happy. Or at least she would be when she got the medicine. It would take her headache away and she could sleep. Hours of dreamless sleep with no nightmares.

"Cathy, sit up. Doc Erin will be here soon.

"Why?" She mumbled, even though she tried to

speak properly, but everything was moving slower than usual. Her body felt like she was dragging it.

"Cathy, do you remember taking the drugs?"

"I took the medicine the doctor gave me." She had. The doctor in New York was right. It did make her feel better. She smiled at him shakily.

"Please, Abe, stop frowning. You look sad."

She giggled, but put her hand over her mouth as he didn't laugh. He looked angrier, if anything. She giggled again, she couldn't help it.

"Stop laughing, Cathy. This is serious. How did you get the medicine?"

"Stop shouting at me." She started crying. Why was he shouting?

"Cathy, think. Where did you get the bottle?"

"From the Doc. I told you. He said I was to take it to feel better."

"He? Did you not see Doc Erin."

"Erin wasn't there. Mrs. Grey said she was busy."

She didn't like it when he was angry. Then he reminded her of someone else. If only she couldn't remember who that was. Her eyelids were closing again. But he wouldn't let her sleep. He kept waking her up.

* * *

"ABE, I think it's a different doctor she is talking about. Doesn't make sense for her to be talking about our Doc. He's usually out visiting the ranches. Doesn't spend much time in town now Doc Erin is here. He doesn't like admitting she's more popular than he is, I guess."

"But she didn't have that bottle yesterday. I'd have seen it. So she had to get it today."

"Well, Doc's here and she can set us straight."

Doc Erin walked in straight over to Cathy, followed by Mary who accused him of trying to drown his wife.

"Mary, be quiet and go fix us some coffee. Please."

Mary left reluctantly, but not before she gave him a dirty look. She obviously blamed him and maybe that was the truth. Cathy was so unhappy she had tried to end it all. What did that say about him?

"Cathy, wake up. Where did you get the medicine?"

"From doctor."

"She keeps repeating that every time I ask her," Abe explained.

"I didn't give to her and she didn't get it from Mrs. Grey or…" Erin picked up the bottle and looked at it closely. "Unless she helped herself."

"So now she is a thief, too?" Abe responded sharply.

"I am not judging her, Abe. I believe she can't help it. The addiction to opium is powerful, much more than we ever believed. She must have been given laudanum by a doctor in New York to help settle her after the tragedy."

"But why would they do that if it was dangerous?

"Why do some people do anything? Her family may have wanted her sedated. Maybe she threatened to harm herself," Erin responded, examining Cathy closely.

"Like she did today?"

"I don't believe she wanted to kill herself today, Abe."

"It sure looks that way."

"No, that is how you think it looks. I am guessing Cathy hasn't been sleeping well. Has she been listless one minute and anxious the next? Is she very ratty with you?"

Abe nodded. It seemed better than expressing in words just how difficult living with Cathy had been over the last few days. At times she was wonderful. She was funny, intelligent, witty. At other times, it was like living with a different person.

"I think the cravings for sleep got to her. I believe she had a nasty experience in town with some people who were unkind to her. She may just have wanted to block everything out of her mind for a while."

"So she will be fine?"

"I didn't say that. Abe, your wife is an addict and for as long as that stuff is in her system there will always be a chance she will lapse back and take more medication. She needs to be locked up so she isn't a danger to herself or to others."

"No."

"But Abe…"

"I said no. Cathy's worst fear is that someone will lock her away in asylum. I refuse to do that. I will look after her."

"You don't have any experience dealing with this type of problem."

"No, he don't, but I do. I'll help him. I have a place higher up in the woods. We will use that."

"But Cookie, you know the risks."

"Yes, Doc more than anyone. But I've done it before and no doubt I will do it again. The only way to get that gal better is to do this. You know it and I knows it. The boy will come, too."

"I ain't a boy. "

"Sorry, son. I didn't mean it like that. Come on, let's get going. We can be there before sundown."

"What will I tell Little Beaver?" Doc Erin asked. "We agreed to keep Cathy on the ranch."

"You tell him to come visit. He knows the cabin. He's been there plenty of times."

Doc Erin nodded. Abe started to pack a bag with some of Cathy's things. She had fallen back asleep, completely oblivious to what was going on around her. She looked so peaceful. He'd failed her. She didn't tell him how bad she was feeling. Why? Did he scare her?

"Wait one minute. I haven't agreed to this. Are you going to trust him with my sister?" Mary protested.

"She's my wife. I take care of my own." His reply came out sharper than he'd meant it to. But Mary ignored him anyway. Her attention was focused on the doc.

"But he nearly drowned her. Made her vomit and everything." Mary continued her protests.

"He did what he needed to do to save her life. Cathy was lucky he did. If he hadn't, we wouldn't be fighting over how to treat her." Cookie's reply brooked no argument.

Mary swayed causing Ben to grab one side and Erin the other.

"Go, I will look after Mary. You come get me if you need me, Cookie," Erin said. "Good luck."

"Thanks, Erin."

Abe gave one last look at Erin's face before she left. Whomever had upset Cathy was in for an ear-bashing from the doctor. He hoped they learned their lesson, because as soon as his wife was better, if anyone upset her again, they would be hearing from him.

CHAPTER 28

He mounted Diamond and Cookie lifted Cathy up into his arms. He followed the older man up into the forests, leaving the ranch behind them. As they moved higher, the forest became denser and the air colder. He shifted Cathy so she was better protected. She was still asleep, but her pulse was stronger than it had been. Just as he was about to ask Cookie how much further they had to ride, Cookie gestured to stop. He couldn't see a cabin but he followed his friend's command.

"We'll walk the rest of the way. The path's a bit rocky, hard on the horses."

It was difficult to secure Cathy to the horse but he did it, hoping they wouldn't have to walk for long. Then he saw it. The cabin was so well-hidden, nobody could find it unless they happened across it by accident or knew it was there.

“I didn’t know you had a place up here.”

“The bunkhouse gets a might crowded at times. When I need some thinking time I head up here. Been a while, though, so I best get to cleaning up. The bed linens are clean so why don’t you put your missus to bed. I will get dinner on soon enough.”

Abe carried Cathy gently into the cabin. It was surprisingly spacious inside with two rooms, one of which was the bedroom. He undressed her gently and put her lying in the large bed in the corner of the room. There was little else but a couple of pegs and a chair. He closed the door but not completely shut in case Cathy woke up, frightened at her new surroundings. He glanced around the main room. In addition to the fireplace there was a sink and small units for the kitchen, a table with two chairs and then a large sofa. In front of the fire was a bearskin similar to the one that lay in their house back at the ranch. The place was relatively clean, too. He was pleased with the sink and taps, as getting water from a spring was too much hard work for his liking. He filled up the kettle and put it to boil over the fire before going outside to find Cookie.

The Indian deputy sheriff was with him. Abe

instinctively checked his gun, causing Little Beaver to give him a cold hard stare.

"Not here to take your wife but if I was, that wouldn't stop me."

"Don't mind Abe, Little Beaver. He's had a tough day. His missus got in some trouble in town."

"Yes, I see her talking to Ma Kelley and knew there would be trouble. I will take the horses back to the ranch for you. You will stay a few days up here?"

Abe looked to Cookie for confirmation. He didn't know how long they would be.

"I have put some things on the porch for you. Mrs. Higgins asked me to bring basket. Said you didn't have time to grab anything."

"Please say thank you for us. Have you any other news?"

"You mean the Pinkertons? They are not coming now. Doc Erin has powerful friends in New York. He got a lawyer for your wife to help fight the man, Archibald Johnston."

"Cathy's cousin. Well, sort of cousin."

Little Beaver took a step toward Abe and held out his hand.

"Cookie and Mick say you good man. I do not wish fight with Cookie and Mick's friend."

Abe shook the hand.

"I will ask the spirits to help your wife heal and for only good times for you both. You have both had much sadness."

Abe stared at the man who on closer examination seemed younger than him but sounded years older.

"Experience makes us both older and wiser, yes?" Little Beaver smiled and then said his goodbyes.

"You need me, send signal."

"Thanks Little Beaver. See you in a few days." Cookie said as the Indian walked away trailing both horses behind him.

"Didn't have a chance to repair the barn and it's too cold to put those horses in a roofless shelter. Little Beaver will look after them."

"He seems like a kind man."

"The best. I would much rather him on our side than be against him. That's for sure."

Abe didn't get a chance to answer as he heard Cathy calling out. He ran to find her struggling to get dressed.

"Where am I? Why are we here? Where's Mary? I need my medicine."

"Cathy, you can't have any more of that stuff. It is poisoning you."

"But I need it. I can't sleep or think or do anything without it."

"Yes you can, and you will. But the next few days will be tough. Do you trust me?"

"I barely know you."

He moved quickly to her side and forced her to look at his face. "Do you trust me?"

She looked him in the eyes before whispering yes.

"I will help you get better. With Cookie's help. He's had experience with this. Together we will get you off this stuff."

"But I need it so bad. Can't I just have a little bit to get through today and we can start tomorrow?"

"No, darling, you can't . We don't have any of that stuff up here and no way to get it. Now let me get you something to eat. You must be hungry."

She didn't reply but sat on the bed, drained of energy.

"Why don't you get back into bed and I will bring it to you?"

"Did you put me to bed before?" she asked, her face crimson.

"Yes."

"You mean, you undressed me?" Her voice rose with panic.

"Cathy, you're my wife. Now, relax and let me get you some food."

Abe prepared a small snack for Cathy, his instincts telling him she wouldn't be able to eat a lot. She didn't. But at least she had some water to drink.

"Thank you for being so kind to me. I really don't deserve it."

"Why not? You haven't done anything wrong."

She went a little pink as she replied. "I have hardly been the easiest to get along with these past few days. I promise I am not always so temperamental."

"Really? I thought all women were like that." He loved teasing her, the way her face lit up as soon as she realized that was what he was doing. It seemed to him for all the money her family had, they never had much fun. She seemed to crave it.

"I mean it, Abe. I am much nicer than this."

"Stop feeling bad and start thinking of getting better. Then we can talk about where we will live."

"Live?"

"Yes, Cathy. We need to make some decisions. I was on my way to New York. I just stopped here to find Cookie and Mick. I wanted Cookie to go see a mutual friend. He is back now and it was time for me to move on. But now..."

"I delayed you. But Abe, why New York?"

"Why not?"

"It is so very different to here. Colorado is so peaceful and pretty. I don't know why anyone would leave to move to a big city."

Now wasn't the right time to tell her his reasons.

"We will talk about it in a few days. Now you need to get some sleep."

"Abe, you don't need to take me with you. You were forced into marrying me. You shouldn't feel responsible for me."

"Cathy O'Malley, I made my vows before God. As far as I'm concerned, you are my wife. We face everything together. Now and in the future."

"Really?"

His insides turned warm at the light of hope in her eyes.

"Yes, really. Now will you please sleep, woman? Some of us have chores to do."

"Yes, husband."

She smiled as she lay back in the bed, her eyes already closing. He leaned over and kissed her lightly on the lips.

Closing the door, he found Cookie sitting at the table a pot of coffee in front of him.

"You not eating, either?"

"No lad, not now. Maybe later. How is she?"

"Calm. Feeling bad about being a burden."

"You know that will change, right?"

Abe wasn't sure what would happen, so he stayed silent.

"The craving will come back. She will do just about anything to get that medicine. You have to be prepared to stop her. Restrain her if necessary."

"I can't tie my wife to the bed," he replied shocked at Cookie for even suggesting it.

"You can and you will. Otherwise we might as well pack up and go to town and let her have as much of that poison as she wants. It isn't going to be pretty, son. The next few days will be a nightmare that never leaves you. But it will be worth it in the end. Just keep telling yourself that.

"Cookie, how many times have you done this?"

"This extreme? Once."

"And did it work?"

"Yes, it did. The man involved has never touched a drop since and he has access to laudanum on a daily basis."

Abe didn't want to ask who it was. He had his suspicions but he didn't want to put Cookie in a difficult situation.

"Now you trust me, don't you, lad?"

"Yes, Cookie, of course. Why are you asking me?"

"Your wife may tell you stories. You got to believe it is the drugs talking."

Abe stared at his friend. "What are you saying?"

"Addicts do strange things, say stranger stuff. They will tell you anything they think will help them get their next taste. She may tell you a lot of lies. You just got to believe they ain't true. You knows I never put a finger on her."

"I know that, Cookie."

"Good."

"Cookie, why did you never marry again?"

"How did you know I was married?"

"Something you said back there. You were, weren't you?"

"Yup."

"What happened?"

"She ran out on me."

"That's rough. Could you not find her?"

"No. Didn't try. No point. She was right to leave."

"Cookie."

"Listen, son, you and I don't share the same beliefs. You believe you made a vow to that girl in there and have to keep it, come what may. Not because of her but because of your God. But I knew I was bad news for my missus. She was better off without me. The war changed me, son, and for the better. Before it ,I was always drinking. Nearly as bad as your Pa."

"You hit your wife?" Abe couldn't keep the disgust from his voice.

"No, but I hurt her just as bad. I was always getting into trouble. Made promises I didn't keep. Then the war came. Nothing about that helped anyone give up drink. But eventually I realized I had to make a choice, quit drinking and start living or dig my own grave. I stopped drinking and ain't had a drink since."

"But your wife?"

"She had gone before I got drafted. She met someone else. He was kind to her. She told me she wanted to get married. So I got a divorce and she left. Ain't seen her since. No idea if she is alive or dead."

"Cookie, I'm sorry."

"Don't be, lad. She was a nice lady, but she wasn't right for me. I wasn't the man she wanted, either. We got married to please our parents. We were too young and foolish to say no. By the time we had our first baby, we hated each other."

"Your child?"

"He died. I guess if he had lived, we may have tried harder but he didn't. There you go. My life story, for what its worth."

"Is that when you started hating God?"

Abe was stunned by the look of horror on Cookie's face.

"Whatever gave you that impression? I love my God."

"But—well, you said…"

"I said you made your vows in a church. My God isn't a church. He is something kind and all powerful. He cares more about what you say and do every day than whether you dress up nice on a Sunday and go to a service."

"Sorry, Cookie. I didn't mean to offend you."

"I know that, lad, but I must be doing something wrong if you thought I was not Christian."

"I hate Him."

"No, you don't. You're just angry. You blame him for what happened to Sally and the baby. Won't be the first to do that and won't be the last."

"But why did he let them die?"

"I can't answer that one, son. Why did he let a nice girl like Cathy end up in the mess she's in? Why allow a good woman like Wilma to live so many years in slavery? Why does he do a lot of things? I have no idea. I just have to believe that he has a plan and he knows better than I do."

"I can't do that."

"You may do in time. You should pray on it."

"Right."

"I'm serious. Little Beaver has had a lot to deal with in his relatively short life. He still deals with prejudice and bigotry on a daily basis. Yet he's smiling. He believes."

"Little Beaver is a Christian?"

"Well, I don't know how you could call him that but he believes in a mighty powerful spirit. Who knows what God is, really? He created all of us, if you read your bible. Anyway, we is getting in way too deep. You think on it, son. Pray on it. Because I am telling you now, that gal of yours in there won't get better without His help. That's the truth, whether you like it or not."

Cookie stood and took off his boots. "I am going go get some shut eye. Reckon you should, too. We could be in for a long night."

"Where will you sleep?" Abe asked.

"Right here, same as always."

As he watched, Cookie pulled the sofa closer to the fire. "This is right comfortable. Goodnight, son."

"Goodnight, Cookie."

Abe went into the bedroom closing he door behind him. Shivering a little at the change in temperature, he stripped to his underclothes and lay in the bed next to his wife. He didn't move in case he woke her. Closing his eyes, he tried to sleep but it was impossible. His thoughts were all jumbled up. Was Cookie right? Was he just angry and really did believe in God? He didn't rightly know what to think anymore.

CHAPTER 29

"You all right, Erin? You been very quiet since you got back from the ranch," Mick asked his wife.

"I am fine, just annoyed. Cathy O'Malley took a drug overdose today."

"Why? I thought she was happy with Abe. Or at least willing to give it a go."

"Nothing to do with Abe, Mick. Seems she came into town and took the bottle from the office. Mrs. Grey didn't notice her taking it. She met Mrs. Shaw and Ma Kelley and they upset her."

"I wish someone would shut those two old women up for good. We have to find a way to drive them out of town."

Erin agreed with her husband but it was pointless

saying so. Nothing was going to happen to those two or Charlie Staunton, for that matter.

"Have you heard back from Mr. Prentice yet?" Mick asked.

"He sent a telegram to say he is looking into it. Not to lose hope, but nothing since."

"Maybe you should send him another one. It would be nice to shut down the gossips once and for all."

"It would be better if Sheriff Willis was here. I love Little Beaver but he doesn't have the same contacts in law enforcement," Erin sighed.

"Sheriff will be back any day now. Where is Cathy?"

"Cookie and Abe took her up to the mountain cabin. Cookie says he has experience of dealing with opium withdrawal."

Erin saw the guarded look on Mick's face.

"What?"

"Nothing."

"Mick what are you hiding from me?"

"Nothing to do with me, love. Not my secret but believe me, Cookie has experience. Cathy should be fine."

"It's not right a girl has to go into the mountains rather than have medical treatment here in town. But if Ma Kelley or the rest of her cronies got word of it, Cathy would never live it down."

"You can trust Cookie, darling. He knows what he is doing. You can only do your best. You are not a miracle worker, you know."

"Hold me, Mick, and tell me everything will work out fine, please."

Mick did just as she asked. Erin only hoped Cathy had found as decent a man as she had.

* * *

THE NEXT MORNING, Erin was planning to go out to the ranch to find out what the latest was with Cathy but she got held up with patients.

"I think Doc has retired."

"At his age he deserves a rest, but at the rate the town is growing we might have to get another doctor. Erin, you can't keep up this pace for long."

Erin was too tired to say anything but she didn't get the chance as the door burst open. Wilma, her two grandchildren and Mrs. Shaw with Bertram were all screaming.

"Quiet down. Someone tell me what is going on," Erin shouted above the noise.

"They cut my boy. Those two evil little witches.

They don't belong here. Send them back to wherever they came from or I will get the law onto them."

"You go get the sheriff right now. He will sort out that devious son of yours. He is not right in the head. Nobody could be that stupid."

"Wilma, settle down. You, too, Mrs. Shaw. Now, will someone please tell me what is going on."

"Bertram said we couldn't be twins. He said his blood was better than Suzy's. So I cut him and Suzy to show him the blood was the same."

Erin exchanged a glance with Emer but neither put their thoughts into words.

"Amy, what did you use?"

"Scissors. Only it weren't sharp enough so I had to sharpen it on a stone first."

"You see, Doc, she is evil. My poor boy, he will be poisoned for sure."

"Mrs. Grey, get Mrs. Shaw out of the office now before I give her a dose of liver oil for her hysterics. Wilma, off you go, too. Get Little Beaver."

Wilma went off looking for the deputy sheriff while Mrs. Grey took a near hysterical Mrs. Shaw away.

"Emer, we have to clean these out and then bandage them up," Erin said in her gravest doctor's voice. "Bertram, you and the girls have been very naughty. You could have been badly hurt. As it is, this is going to sting a lot."

"I don't want it to hurt."

"Stop being such a cry baby, you silly boy. You are never going to be a man if you let a bit of a sting scare you," Amy shouted at Bertram.

"I will, too. Just you watch me."

"I could watch for the rest of my life. You're only ever going to be a boy. You are never going to be sensible like me and Suzy."

"Amy, you didn't show much sense doing this. You could have given your sister and Bertram blood poisoning. I am not at all happy with you three and I doubt your teacher is, either," Erin said sharply.

"What is going on in here?"

Erin looked up to see Little Beaver frowning at the children. He looked very fierce. Suzy hid behind Amy. Or at least she tried to.

"Your teacher told me you have all been very naughty. Bertram, I told you the price if you got into trouble again."

"Wasn't me this time, it was them. Honest it was. You just ask them."

"It was me, not either of them. I wanted to prove him wrong. I didn't realize what I was doing was bad,"

Amy said, a groveling expression of innocence on her face.

Erin saw Little Beaver was fighting hard to keep his strict face. Amy looked like butter wouldn't melt in her mouth.

"Amy, what's your least favorite chore?"

"Washing windows."

"That's a big lie, Amy. You love that job. She hates peeling vegetables and weeding."

"You are supposed to be my sister. What did you tell him that for?"

"Cause you deserve to be punished. What you did was wrong. You should say you are sorry."

"See, I told you. Even your own sister thinks you are evil."

"You shush your mouth, Bertram Shaw. I do not. I think you are horrible. You never think before you open that big fat mouth of yours. I hate you. I hate both of you," Suzy said, tears sliding down her face.

"Emer, can you take Suzy into the other room and tend to her cut. Thankfully it isn't deep, although it's deeper than Bertram's which is just a scratch. But I don't think Suzy needs to hear any more of her sister's nonsense."

Amy sent Erin a dirty look, but Suzy sent one of gratitude.

"I am going to tell your mother to send you to the orphanage for a month," Little Beaver told Bertram. "You and Amy can weed the garden for Samuel and if I hear one word of complaint, I will make it two."

"My ma won't let you tell me what to do."

"She will because if you and your ma don't start listening to my deputy, I am going to put you both in jail. I will send you away to a school for badly behaved boys and you wont see your ma for six months. Do you hear me?"

"Yes."

"Yes what?"

"Yes, sir, Sheriff Willis."

"Now, somebody get Mrs. Shaw home or I will lock her up for causing a public disturbance."

Mrs. Shaw didn't need any assistance. She was gone when Erin turned to look for her. Bertram followed in her wake.

Wilma came back into the clinic to collect her grandchildren. "Erin, I am so sorry. I don't know what to say. I am so ashamed."

"Girls, come here and apologize to your Grammy. She doesn't need you two causing her problems like this. You hear me?"

"Yes, Doc Erin."

"What do you say?"

"Sorry, Grammy. Sorry, Doc Erin. Sorry, Sheriff."

"All right, off you go now," Erin said.

"Do I really got to do weeding with Bertram?"

"Yes, you do, Amy and Suzy is not to help you. You got into this mess on your own. You can get out of it on your own," Erin confirmed.

"Oh darn."

"Amy! Wait till I get you home and you are going to feel my hand across your backside. I'm going to fill that mouth of yours with soapy water. Just you watch me. You never to use that language again, you hear?"

Sheriff Willis and Mrs. Grey roared laughing at the sight of Wilma dragging a willful Amy up the street. Erin was amused, too, but she wasn't about to laugh. She had yet to see what type of child Michelle would turn into and she wasn't in the mood for tempting fate. She sure was glad the Sheriff was back. He may be able to help keep Cathy out of trouble.

CHAPTER 30

"Morning, son. How is she?"

"Still asleep. Should she be still sleeping?" Abe asked.

"I guess she did take rather a large amount. Just make sure she's breathing. It will easier for everyone if she's asleep."

That was the second or third time Cookie had mentioned how difficult the next few days would be. He hoped his friend was exaggerating.

"Morning."

"Little Beaver, you're back already," Cookie said.

Abe looked up as the Indian approached with two horses.

"Sheriff is back. I told him where you were. Came

back with your horse, Cookie. You still riding out today?"

"Aye. Just let me rinse this and I will be right with you."

"Wait, Cookie. You're leaving?"

"Abe, this is something you and Cathy got to do together. There is nothing I can do that you can't and your missus will be more comfortable if it is just you that sees her. I wont be far away. If you need me, fire a shot. Someone will come."

"Good luck, Abe," Little Beaver added as the two men walked away. Abe just stared, too shocked to comment.

It was just him and Cathy now. That thought didn't bring him comfort. What if he let her down? What if he couldn't save her and she died.

No point in thinking like that. Might as well get the chores done while she's sleeping.

It was a couple more hours before Cathy woke. She begged him for more medicine and when he said there wasn't any, she didn't believe him. She went through the cabin, opening every drawer or door she could find. It looked like thieves had ransacked the place by the time she was finished. Then she turned on him. One minute she was all nice as pie, the next she was tearing at his face, his eyes. All the time begging him for just a little bit.

"I just need a tiny spoonful. Not even a full spoon. Just a little bit. Why won't you give it to me? You don't care about me."

At first he tried to reason with her, but soon gave up. He tried his best to ignore her as she yelled and screamed. Now, he understood why Cookie had insisted on them going away from normal folks. When Cathy was better, she would be mortified at the way she had carried on. She certainly didn't need anyone reminding her. Even if she didn't remember, it would have given the children nightmares to hear a grown woman scream and beg like that. She sounded like she was being attacked and tortured.

He ended up tying her to the bed, the tears pooling in his eyes as she begged and pleaded with him for some drugs. She chaffed at the bounds so much her skin turned raw. He clipped her nails so she wouldn't shred her own skin. He tried to get her to drink water but she wouldn't. Every so often she passed out, but it didn't last long. Her body was twitching as the drugs worked their way out of her. He kept the cabin hot in the hope by sweating she would get it out faster, but really he had no idea what he was doing.

Every so often he found little gifts outside. A basket of freshly caught fish, a loaf of bread, some cookies. These reminders he wasn't alone and had friends thinking of him helped a lot. He cooked, cleaned, sponged her down, stripped the bed, remade it. Every day was the same. By the third day he was exhausted, yet she seemed to be gaining energy. He found himself praying. Not saying the prayers by rote as he had done as a child but talking to God and asking him for help. It didn't appear as if he was listening.

CHAPTER 31

The next day, Sheriff Willis called to the Haven. Mick was home alone, Nora having taken Michelle over to the orphanage to see Wilma. Mick opened the door, surprised to find the sheriff standing there.

"Come on in, Sheriff. Erin said she'd seen you."

"That's a mess in New York. I sent a couple of telegrams off to some fellas I know. They will get back to me with the inside story. In the meantime, Little Beaver has checked on Cathy and she is doing all right."

"Is she back on the ranch yet?" Mick asked.

"No, not yet. It takes some time."

Mick remembered his manners. "I got fresh coffee on. Might even be able to rustle up some cookies."

"Thanks Mick but I don't think I can eat. Stomach isn't too good."

"You talk to Erin?"

"I don't need no doctor. I need...Oh, forget it."

The sheriff turned around and went to head out the door. Mick stopped him by putting a hand on his shoulder.

"Come in and have some coffee. I got a letter from Mollie yesterday. She loves Santa Fe. Says the people are real nice to her. She's back in school. Wants to be a doctor, just like Erin. That's something, isn't it."

Mick knew he was talking too much but he was so surprised finding the sheriff at his door, he wasn't sure what to say. Did he want to talk about Cathy?

"You know Cathy, Mary Sullivan's sister turned up in town while you were away."

"Aye. Little Beaver filled me in. That is some funny situation right there. The law can't be too worried about her if they ain't sending anyone after her. Something fishy about the whole thing, if you ask me."

"So you don't mind Abe—he's her husband now—taking her up to the Cookie's cabin on the mountain."

"From what I hear about the little lady, that's the best place for her. After the war, I saw many men fight that poison. Not a pretty sight. I think I ran into this Abe's brother in Leadville. A guy by the name of Jude."

"Yes, he told me Jude had become a sheriff. Reckon next to Little Beaver, he is about the youngest sheriff around. Funny, when I met him years back, I would have put him in the cells in the jailhouse. He was a little tyke but he has grown into a fine man."

The sheriff smiled, which worried Mick even more. Braddon Willis was not known for smiling or cracking jokes. "Sheriff, what can I do for you? I get the impression this isn't just a social call."

"Mick, you know how to dance right?"

"I do okay. I don't stand on the ladies' feet. Why?"

"You goin' to the wedding Saturday week."

More confused than ever, Mick said, "Yes, Of course. I couldn't miss Wilma's wedding. But I'll be dancin' with Erin."

"I know that, you big lummox. I want to dance with a lady, too, but I—well, I don't know how."

"Don't tell me you want me to show you?" Mick hoped he didn't. He wouldn't feel right holding the sheriff by the hand and waltzing him around the room.

"What do you think I am? I wondered if you knew if any of the ladies would teach me to dance. I thought your Erin might do it but I guess she's too busy. All the ladies in town are too busy."

"What about Mrs. Grey?" Mick said innocently,

while stirring the coffee. This conversation was getting rather embarrassing.

The silence hit him. He turned to look at the sheriff, surprised to find him bright red.

"What did I say? Oh, Mrs. Grey." Suddenly Mick knew why the sheriff was here. He should have seen the signs earlier. Erin had commented there seemed to be an attraction between Mrs. Grey and Willis. "You want to court Mrs. Grey?"

"I never said that. Why you jumping to conclusions? You are worse than an old woman." Sheriff puffed up.

"You do, you old goat. I never thought I would see the day. We best get you out to the Sullivan ranch. Mrs. H will help you learn to dance. Reckon Miss Mary would teach you a couple of the Irish reels if you ask nicely."

"Now, Mick, don't you be getting ideas and spreading rumors. Or I will put that backside of yours in the cells."

"That's not a nice way to treat your best man, is it?"

"What? Ah, now, I knew I shouldn't have said anything. You ain't going to let this go, are ye?"

"Nope! Now, are we going out to the ranch and speaking to Mrs. H or aren't we?"

Mick hid a smile as the sheriff tried to work out

which was worse—showing himself up by dancing all over Mrs. Grey's toes or admitting to the ladies at the ranch he had to learn how to dance.

"Listen, Sheriff, it will do Mary a favor. She is beside herself worrying about her sister. If she had this distraction, it would make her day go faster."

"Hmph" was the only response he got but he took it for a yes. He wanted to speak to Davy, anyway. Mr. Prentice was interested in buying beef from Davy if the price was right and he could supply the quantities he needed. Mr. Prentice believed a number of his contacts would be interested in dealing with the ranches in Clover Springs but they would prefer to meet Davy in person. Davy hated big cities more than Mick did so he wasn't at all sure the man would go to New York.

"Sheriff, I got to bring Robbie in on your secret."

"Who's Robbie?"

"Robbie Fenton, going to be in charge of the new hotel he is building in Clover Springs. I need to introduce him to Davy and get some business dealings sorted."

"This trip to New York seems to have gone to your head, Mick Quinn. Big hotels and business deals."

"I am still the same guy you know, Sheriff. Don't

you worry about that. Robbie's a good sort. You'll like him."

* * *

ROBBIE AGREED to go the Sullivan ranch with them. Robbie and the sheriff got on very well and the day went better than Mick had anticipated. Davy wasn't keen on going to New York but Robbie suggested Mr. Prentice would come to Clover Springs.

After they had spoken about business, Mick asked the ladies for help with his dancing.

"With Wilma's big day coming up, there is bound to be dancing and last time I danced with Erin, I nearly broke her toes. Can you help me become a better dancer?"

"Sure we can Mick. You just need to count out the steps to the music," Mary said kindly.

"Make sure you keep it a surprise from Erin. I don't want her to know I had to take lessons. I bribed the sheriff into coming with me. Erin will just assume we are talking about Cathy's case." Mick saw the look of relief on the sheriff's face. Poor man, had he really believed he would tell the women of his intentions?

"Sheriff, do you think they will still come looking for Cathy?"

"I don't rightly know, Mrs. Sullivan, but we always protect our own. Your sister is one of us now, so unless they come with the correct legal paperwork, she isn't going anywhere. I said to Mick I have some suspicions about what's going on in New York. Seem to be taking their time to make their way here. So don't you fret, we will sort it out."

"Thanks, sheriff. Are you going to learn how to dance, too?"

"Well, Mick thought it best if I helped make up the numbers."

Mick had to turn away so he wouldn't laugh at the innocent expression on the sheriff's face.

CHAPTER 32

Cathy woke up completely disoriented. Raising her head, she groaned. Everything felt so heavy. When she moved her limbs, it was like they were stuck in molasses. She needed a drink of water—her mouth was all dry and sandy. She tried to sit up but found she was tied to the bed. Terrified, she worked at the ropes but they didn't loosen. She looked around her, not wanting to scream in case it brought back in whomever had done this to her. She didn't recognize the cabin.

"Morning. How are you feeling?"

"What are you doing? Why do you have me tied to the bed?"

He pulled out a knife, causing her to shrink back into the pillow. Was this it? The end?

He sliced through the binds, freeing her. She sat up, warily watching him and the knife. He put it away.

"Sorry, Cathy. It was for your own good."

She didn't know what to believe. She couldn't remember a lot. Some hazy images and wanting something so bad she was prepared to do anything. She looked at him closer.

"That's a nasty scratch on your face. Who did you upset?"

"You."

"What? I didn't do that. I'd never hurt anyone," Cathy denied.

"You did, but it wasn't your fault. It was the drugs."

Drugs? What was he talking about? She looked around her again. "Where am I?"

"We moved up to Cookie's cabin for a few days. Been here about a week now."

"Just the two of us?" she squeaked, pulling the covers up to her chest.

"Yes. Although Cookie and Little Beaver have been helping. They have left us food almost every day."

"Why?"

"I was busy."

"Doing what?"

He gave her a cup of water. She drank greedily.

"Cathy, the last few days. Do you remember any of it?"

She stared at him, trying hard to remember stuff but nothing was forthcoming. There was an uneasy feeling in her stomach that grew with every minute. She knew at some level she had done something, but what? She couldn't be sure.

"I was ill?"

"You were recovering from taking too much medicine. I need to know, Cathy. Did you do it on purpose?"

"What?"

"Were you so unhappy you wanted to die?"

"Die? You mean, did I try to kill myself? No. That's a sin."

"Yes, I know it is, but I also know what it is like to feel you have no hope, no life and no reason for going on."

She studied his face, sensing he was being honest with her in the hope she would return the favor.

"I just wanted to sleep. Not forever. Just for a while. I was so tired and hurt and angry. Then those ladies..." she couldn't continue.

"What ladies?"

"Some women in town. I heard them speaking about me. You know you should never eavesdrop on other people's conversation. You never hear anything good about yourself."

He took her hand, gently caressing her wrist with his thumb. She gulped at the sensations moving through her body. She wanted him to stop, yet didn't at the same time.

"They said I was responsible for my parents' death. They suggested it was Davy's money that was keeping me out of jail."

"That's nonsense. If the police wanted to arrest you they would have done that already. They haven't so quit worrying. It will all work out."

"How are you so sure?"

"Doc Erin has friends in New York. One of them hired some Pinkertons to investigate the accident. Another is on the police force. They will prove you were innocent. Doc Erin thought it was a bit fishy that you weren't arrested. She thinks, and I agree, it was all rumors."

"But why would anyone say something so horrible?"

"Cathy, what was the situation between you and Archibald Johnston? Were you in love?" he asked.

She shook her head. They weren't even in like. She certainly didn't like him. She thought he was shallow, mean-minded and dull. He appeared to hate her, a feeling he'd had since they were young.

"No. It wasn't a love match. I didn't even know there was anything said about us being married. Then Archibald showed me the letter my father wrote. He appointed Archibald my guardian and suggested we marry. He didn't think I would be able to cope managing his estate, I guess."

"Archibald was the one who first gave you the medicine?"

"No, a doctor gave me that. Archibald asked him to look after me because I was so upset about Mama and Papa. I had nightmares about drowning and everything. And then when I found Mary's letters, I felt so betrayed. Like everything I had ever known was a lie. I guess I had some sort of breakdown." Cathy fidgeted. "Are they going to put me in an asylum?"

"Nobody is going to do that."

"But if they think I tried to kill myself and if that doctor says I had a breakdown, then surely nobody can stop them."

"I can and I will. You're my wife now, Cathy. Nobody can hurt you. This Archibald guy has no control over you."

She tried to smile but the tears came instead.

"Are you unhappy?"

"No, I'm crying because I am so relieved. He took me to visit the hospital for the insane once. He insisted we see the patients and the wards." She shuddered.

She saw his hands clench.

"I think it was his way of making me do as he wanted."

"What a pig. You are best off without him."

She wanted to ask him to hold her, but suddenly found she was too shy. Which was ridiculous, as if what he said was true and they had been here for a few days, he had seen and touched every part of her already. Her face grew hot.

"Are you feeling sick again? You have gone very red."

"No, just thinking," she squeaked.

He grinned as understanding spread over his face.

"You have nothing to worry about. I swear I was a perfect gentleman."

"Thank you."

"It was very hard, though. You have a lovely…"

"Abe! Stop it."

"I will on one condition."

"What?" She wondered if he would demand a kiss?

"You have a bath. You don't smell too good, Mrs. O'Malley."

"Oh, you…" She picked up her pillow and hit him

with it. He roared with laughter before telling her he was going to boil some water.

She lay there for a few minutes after he left, wondering about him. He'd been so kind and caring. He'd gotten angry when she'd spoken about Archibald. He'd claimed her as his wife more than once. Did he want a real marriage? Did she?

CHAPTER 33

Abe sat outside, waiting for Cathy to finish her bath. Even though he had seen her in all her glory, it was different now she was awake. She seemed to be doing okay. He wondered how long it would be before the cravings returned.

He got up to chop some wood when his thoughts went wandering where they shouldn't. She was his wife so it was natural, but still it wasn't as if they were a real couple. She had agreed to the marriage to avoid being locked up. He had agreed to it because…why had he agreed to it? Was it really just down to his friends asking or was it more personal than that. If he was honest, he'd found her very attractive from the beginning. She had beautiful eyes, but it was more than just physical. She'd woken a need in him. An instinct to protect her. She seemed to reach inside of him and just squeeze his heart.

He chopped faster. If anyone could read his thoughts, they would be locking him up for going soft.

"Abe, I am done. It's safe for you to come in now."

He walked indoors to find her in front of the fire, trying to get the tangles out of her hair. He'd been shocked by how long it actually was, that first night he'd seen it. He emptied the bath and put the tin container outside. Closing the door, he found her still working her way through her hair. Wordlessly he took the brush from her and started combing out the tangles. Her hair was smooth and silky. He imagined how it would feel against his…

"Abe, thank you."

"For what?"

"For all this. I am sorry I took that medicine."

"Next time you feel real bad, come talk to me."

"There won't be a next time. I will never take that stuff again."

He stopped combing and sat down on the rug beside her. Putting his arm around her shoulders, he drew her closer.

"Cathy, Doc Erin and Cookie both said there might be a next time."

When she moved to protest, he shushed her with a

finger against her lips. "Nobody is saying you are weak, only that drug is powerful and it will tempt you. Again and again. We just have to work together to stop things ever getting so bad you feel it's the only answer. Okay?"

She stared into the fire, a look of terror on her face.

"Look at me, Cathy. Think about what you did already. You knew something was wrong, that someone was giving you drugs. You got out and came to Clover Springs all by yourself. Doc Erin says you were almost wasting away yet you still wouldn't eat or drink for fear of taking that stuff again. You did all that once. You can do it again. Only this time, you won't have to starve. I won't let anyone, Archibald or anyone else, near you. I promise."

"Can you be sure of that? He has lots of money and is very powerful."

"I don't have money but we have friends here. I would like to see a namby pamby city boy try to survive out here."

"But he knows I am in Clover Springs."

He drew her closer and kissed her gently on the head. "Then we will move. Somewhere he doesn't know us. Our friends here won't tell him where you've gone. Cathy Johnston can just disappear."

"Leave Mary and everyone again?"

"We don't have to go far. We can stay in Colorado and visit or they can come visit us."

She lay back against him, her face flickering as she digested what he had said.

"Cathy, do you trust me?"

"Yes," she whispered.

He leaned down and took her mouth with his. Pulling her closer, he melded her to his body, not hiding his need for her.

"I'd like you to become my wife. For real."

"I'd like that, too," she whispered back, not looking at his face. He smiled as he kissed her. He had to be gentle and take things slowly.

CHAPTER 34

The next few days were some of the happiest Cathy could remember. She and Abe were getting to know each other in every way possible. They bickered a little, but never for long. Cathy found each day she woke feeling better. She started to believe Abe was right—she could win her battle with the drug.

This morning, Cathy tried to make some coffee but she couldn't find any. She kicked a couple of things as she moved in the relative darkness.

"Do I smell breakfast?" her husband teased from the bed.

"No. I can't find the coffee."

"Good job I didn't marry you for your cooking talents."

"Sorry. I just wanted to do something nice for you. But I've got a lot to learn."

"Leave it and come back to bed."

"Abe!"

"Wife, get back to bed now. You promised to obey me, remember."

She put the pot down and almost jumped into the bed beside him. He cradled her in his arms.

"What do you think about us going back to the ranch today?"

"Today? Do we have to?" She hated sounding like a child but she didn't want this to end. She was getting to know her husband and enjoying the process.

"Can't we stay another day or two?"

"I thought you would hate it up here. It's not exactly luxury. "

"I think that's part of the charm. I never thought I would be happy in such a small place, but I am."

"We have to face the real world sooner or later."

"Can't we make it later, please?"

"Well, you could convince me," he whispered, putting on a rakish accent. It made her laugh.

"That wasn't quite what I had in mind," he responded, sounding a little sulky. She kissed his bare shoulder, then his neck before finding his mouth.

"Better?" she asked in between kisses

"Much…" he said rolling her over as he folded her close to his body.

"Anyone home?" Cookie's voice broke into their little world.

"Darn it, anyway. Where did he come from?"

She couldn't answer, she was too busy laughing at the look on his face. Cookie's voice sounded once again.

"You best go see what he wants," she prompted.

"Why can't you go?"

"Be serious, Abe. I can't go out like this."

"Might make him leave faster. Oh, okay, don't look at me like that." He rolled out of bed and dressed quickly. "I'm coming," he yelled to Cookie. Then he bent down and kissed her quickly "We will have to take this up again when he leaves."

She hid under the covers so Cookie wouldn't hear her giggling. She was so happy but scared, too. Would she be punished for feeling so good after everything that had happened?

* * *

"Morning. You're early." Abe greeted Cookie.

"Grumpy, aren't we? And it's almost lunchtime, in case you hadn't noticed."

Abe didn't say anything. He hadn't realized it was so late.

"I didn't mean to butt in on you guys, but I got news."

Cathy had come out of the cabin, but neither man seemed to hear her approach.

"Bad news?" she said, but her voice came out all squeaky.

"Why don't you make some coffee and I will tell ya," Cookie said.

"I'll make it. Cathy hasn't got the hang of the fire yet. She is more used to stoves."

"Mrs. Higgins sent up an apple pie and some cookies. Said the fresh air would give you an appetite."

Abe couldn't meet Cathy's eyes for fear of embarrassing her. He busied himself making the coffee while his wife got some dishes and clean mugs. The three of them sat down.

Cookie took his time drinking and eating before Abe lost patience.

"Come on, Cookie, tell us. The both of us are on a knife edge wanting to know."

"I got good news and some not-so-good news."

Abe felt Cathy reaching for him. He held onto her hand tightly.

"The good news is that the police have confirmed

you are no longer a person of interest, ma'am. Seems the boat wasn't river-worthy or something. But nothing you could have done would have changed the outcome. Your father threw you off the boat and then tried to rescue your mother. But it was too late. They have ruled your parents' death an accident and have dropped the charges of fraud and theft."

"That's fantastic. Hear that, Cathy?"

Cathy's eyes were glued to Cookies face.

"What's the bad news?" she asked.

Cookie took a rather noisy drink from his coffee. "Well, I guess it's best I told you and you don't hear it from the gossips."

"Cookie, out with it.

"Seems this Archibald fella you been talking about, he got a judge to rule that your adoption was never legal. Therefore, you are not the heiress to the Johnston estate."

"Let me guess, that conniving little snake is?"

"Yes, Abe, he is."

"What do you mean it wasn't legal?" Cathy asked him. "How could they adopt me if it wasn't allowed?"

"Seems your parents made a large donation to the convent and the sisters had them sign some papers. But for whatever reason those papers were never put through the court system. So in the eyes of the law, you were never adopted. Your real, legal name is Catherine Ryan.

Cathy pushed her chair back suddenly, causing it to fall over.

"My parents were never mine. It was all a lie? Everything?"

"Cathy, it doesn't matter. You don't need their money or anything else. You said yourself, all we could ever need is right here."

"Can't you see? It's wrong, all of it."

Abe couldn't see. What was wrong? Was she upset at losing the money? He guessed he might be if it was him.

"Cathy, we can fight it if you want. Not sure how much good it will do but we could go to New York."

"No, we can't. You and me are done, finished."

And with that she ran.

Abe looked at Cookie, who was staring into the fire.

"What do I do now?"

"She'll come back. It's been a shock to her. Seems that toad Archibald planned on getting the money one way or another. He announced their engagement but all the time he was trying to get the adoption overturned."

"How did you find all this out?"

"Doc Erin got a letter from her friend, Mr. Prentice. He's been investigating everything in New York. Hired a couple of Pinkertons. Found out a lot of stuff. None of it relevant to Cathy, at least not anymore."

Cookie stood up. "I best be off and leave you to it. Have patience with her, son. She just found out everything she believed for years was a lie. That's bound to shake her up a little. Stay here and work it out. While you can. Back down there, the gossips are having a field day, as you can just imagine."

"Did you bring any good news with you?" Abe said as he walked Cookie down the hill a little.

"There's a big party this Saturday. Wilma and Zack are celebrating their wedding and those friends of Doc Erin's have arrived from New York. The whole town is likely to be there."

Cookie turned to take a look back at the cabin, but Cathy had yet to return. "Go easy with her, lad. You two seem to have been getting along well."

That had to be the understatement of the year. They had been getting on great, but now the future wasn't looking so rosy.

CHAPTER 35

He watched until Cookie was out of sight and then he walked slowly back to the cabin. Cathy hadn't come back. He walked toward the river behind the cabin. She liked coming down here, said the water helped her think. He found her sitting on a rock, tears streaming down her face He reached for her

"Go away."

"Cathy, come on. Talk to me. "

"I said leave me alone."

"Cathy, I am your husband."

"Don't you see? You aren't. You married Cathy Johnston. She doesn't exist. I don't exist. I don't even know what to call myself anymore."

He pulled her up and into his arms despite her

protests and walked her back to the cabin. He put her on the bed and then went back to close and lock the cabin door.

"Cathy, it doesn't matter what your last name is. We are married in the eyes of God. That means we deal with this together. I am not leaving you. Not now, not ever."

"But why would you want me? I have nothing. I don't even have a right to use my name."

"I never married you for your parents' money or New York houses. I can't miss what we never had." The joke fell a bit flat. He put his arm out to her and took her hand, stroking it.

"Cathy, I admit. When I married you it was for the wrong reasons." At the suspicious look on her face, he quickly continued. "I did it because Mick asked me to. I owed him for helping me over the years. I didn't care who I married, not really."

"If this is your way of helping me, I don't think it's working."

"No, listen to me. The first time I picked you up, when you fainted that time, I had a funny feeling about you. An instinct that you and me—well, we were meant to meet. I know it sounds like something out of a penny dreadful but its true."

She didn't say anything but he took that as a good

sign. At least she was listening.

"You looked so beautiful at the wedding, but your eyes were full of pain. I wanted to take that away. I wanted to make you feel better and then maybe, just maybe, I would start feeling something again, too. The first night at the house on the ranch, when you wouldn't sleep without me beside you..."

Her eyes dropped to the floor as her face turned crimson.

He put a finger under her chin and gently made her look at him. "That was the first time in a long time I felt needed. Wanted. I had a reason to be here." He stopped, thinking he might be scaring her but she seemed to be listening intently.

"Then over the next few days as I got to know you, I wanted to know you better. You make me laugh, Cathy. Not because I laugh at you but with you. You have an ability to light up a whole room. You are kind and caring.

"You make me sound like a saint," she retorted, possibly because his words seemed to embarrass her.

"Well, unless saints are also moody, cranky and can't cook, I don't think you qualify."

She nudged him but he saw she was trying not to smile.

"I know we don't know each other very well but

we can work on that. We are both young and healthy. We have good friends nearby. You have a sister who adores you, who never stopped loving you. We have more, much more than a lot of people."

"But instead of an heiress, you got a drug addict."

"I never expected to marry someone rich and you are so much more than what you describe. You became addicted because someone took advantage of you when they should have been caring for you. What sort of twisted mind does that to someone who is part of their family?" He'd love to get his hands on Archibald Johnston but it was probably good that opportunity was unlikely to arise.

"But I'm not. We aren't related. We were never family."

"Cathy, your parents saw you as their daughter and if that man had any honor he wouldn't treat you so badly, if only for their sake."

"Not everyone thinks like you Abe."

"I don't care what anyone else thinks. I care about what you think. Do you believe we are married?"

She stared at him for a few seconds. "Yes," she said miserably

"Well, then. We go see Father Molloy, get him to do the blessing again with your correct name and all is well with the world."

"But how are we going to live? I don't have any skills and you...well, you don't seem to have any money. You said you were going East and I never want to go back there."

She had a point. He could make do as a single man but he wasn't alone anymore. He had a wife and maybe in time they would have a family. He had a mother and sister back in Noelle. He had land, too. He'd spent years clearing it with a view to farming. Most of the hard work was done. His ma would help Cathy learn how to run a household. But would she want to live in the house he had shared with Sally? He closed his eyes. Thinking of Sally didn't bring the same pain as it had. She would always be part of his life but somehow he knew she wouldn't have expected him to live alone forever. She'd been gone over a year now. It was a bit soon, but then everything about this marriage had been different to how it should be.

"Abe?"

"Sorry. I was wool-gathering. Let's sit in front of the fire with the picnic Cookie brought us. Then we can plan our future."

She grabbed his hand and let him pull her into his arms to give her a hug. It took no time at all to set out their meal.

* * *

"CATHY, you know I was married before, don't you?"

She stiffened, withdrawing her hand from his. She wrapped her arms around her knees. "No. You never said and I didn't think to ask."

"Oh. Well, I was. Her name was Sally and we had a baby, a girl. She and the child died in a smallpox outbreak about a year ago now. I couldn't function when they died. All I did was drink and be mad at the world."

"You must have loved her very much," she whispered. What was he doing married to her now? Was she some sort of replacement for his other family? Exactly like she had been a replacement for Mama and Papa's real children.

"I grew up with Sally. She was a part of the family almost before we got married. I guess if she hadn't died we would have grown old together. We were happy." He took her hand, pulling it free from where she had it wrapped around her. "You have nothing to worry about. I won't compare you to Sally. You and her—well, it would be like comparing an apple to a berry. You are totally different."

"I am sorry about your wife and daughter," she said formally. What was she supposed to say? Why had he waited to tell her until now? Just as she thought they had a chance at happiness. "I think we should go back to the ranch tomorrow. Do you mind if I go to bed now? I feel very tired."

"Sure thing. I'll just clean up here and then I'll join you."

"Actually, I would prefer to sleep alone. It's been an upsetting, long day."

She didn't wait for his answer but pulled the door shut behind her. Not bothering to undress, she climbed under the covers, totally miserable. She hadn't realized quite how much she liked him until now. Maybe she even loved him. Why else would it feel as if her heart was breaking in two? It was like when she'd lost her parents, maybe even worse.

* * *

ABE STOOD STARING at the door. What had he said? Was she upset about Sally? Hadn't he made it clear that what they had was different? He was tempted to push his way past the door and insist she speak to him. To lie on the bed beside her, but that would be wrong. Maybe she just needed time to think about what Cookie had said. He poked the fire before throwing a couple more logs onto it. It looked like a long and rather uncomfortable night.

When he woke the next morning, Cathy had her bags packed and the bed stripped. She had bundled the sheets up together. "I will bring these back to the ranch so I can wash them. Then I can give them to Cookie to bring them back here."

He didn't say anything. She looked as bad as he felt, with black circles under her eyes. She was avoiding his gaze as if she was a stranger and not his wife.

"Cathy, about yesterday—"

"Do you mind if we don't talk? I have a horrible headache. I really just want to get back to the ranch and see Mary and the little ones. I've missed them and Ben."

"Oh, right."

He packed up the last of the things they had brought with them. Some items were too big to carry back.

"We don't have the horses, so will have to walk."

"That's fine. It will help my head."

He stared after her as she started walking. She had no idea how long the walk would take and he was certain she wasn't used to walking long distances, but it seemed she was desperate to get away from him.

CHAPTER 36

Cathy kept walking in what she hoped was the general direction of the ranch. She was too upset to see properly, the tears blinding her vision. She wanted to scream at him, to ask him why he had consummated their marriage when he didn't care for her. But then if he didn't care, why had he brought her up here? But Mama cared and look what she did. She hid the letters from Mary. People didn't behave the way you expected. Maybe it was her. She was just one of those who were never destined to have a proper family. Mary had been kind and welcoming, but she had a family of her own now. A husband who loved her and children. Beautiful children. She couldn't stop the sob escaping.

* * *

"RIGHT, that's enough. Put that stuff down, Cathy O'Malley, and tell me what's wrong."

"Noting. I just want to get back to the ranch."

"Cathy, talk to me. After everything, after these last few days, I thought you trusted me."

"Why did you sl..." She couldn't ask him. She couldn't even look at him.

"Are you asking me why I lay with you? I am a man and you are a very attractive woman."

"So anyone would have done, so long as you got what you wanted."

"I wouldn't dignify that with a response, only you seem to have got it into your head that I don't care for you. Cathy, you are wrong. I care for you a whole lot. I love you."

Her head swung up at his words.

"I would swear it on my life, but that's not a good thing to do. Cathy, I never met anyone like you. I want to get to know you better but already you have stolen my heart. I never believed in love at first sight and I don't think that's what happened to us. But these past two weeks, you have given me so much joy. You gave me reason to live again. To wake up in the morning wanting to share my day with you. I never thought I would feel anything for anyone. You make me angry, mad as a hornet, and at the same time you make me laugh. You, Cathy. I don't care what your second name is or whether your adoption was real or not. I want you, in my life, in my bed, to share everything with me. Good times and bad."

She couldn't believe him. She wanted to, but…

"Cathy I have seen you at your worst and I still want you in my life. Can't you just open your eyes and see?" He wanted to shake her. How could she not see?

"Something brought us together, God or fate or whatever you want to believe. But there is a reason I was in Clover Springs at the same time you came here. It was not pure chance."

"But what of Sally and your daughter?" she whispered.

"They will always be part of me, but just because they are doesn't mean you come second best. You are my wife."

"You aren't just saying that because you feel sorry for me?"

"Sorry for you? You enjoyed a lifestyle most people can only dream about. You have seen foreign places nobody else in Clover Springs will ever see. I am sorry your parents died so tragically and they didn't get a chance to explain about the letters. But I have my own theory on that."

"Which is?"

"Cathy, maybe your ma was worried she would lose you forever. She may have believed the ties between family are so strong that if you knew Mary was married and could provide you with a home, you would leave. She was probably terrified. You said she showed you lots of love and affection, so it would be out of character for her to hide the letters to be mean."

He took a step toward her and held his arms out. "Darling, please give us both a chance. We could be happy together. I will cook every day if it makes you smile."

"You will?" She went into his arms and kissed him fiercely.

"Well, only until you learn to do it. Cooking's women's work, you know."

"Abe O'Malley, that's using false pretenses."

He swept her off her feet and into his arms. "There is nothing false about us, Cathy. Nothing at all." He followed his declaration with a kiss that seared her soul.

* * *

After some time, they started walking again, but this time hand in hand.

"Abe, you know you said you had land somewhere near your ma and sister. Do you miss them?"

"Ma and Cara? Yes. Feel guilty, too, leaving them to it. I mean, I have brothers and all, but I am the eldest and I been looking after Ma since I was about fourteen."

"Would you like to go back there?"

"To visit?"

"To live. I wouldn't mind. I can come visit with Mary and she can come to us. If you want."

He leaned over and kissed her on the nose. "Let's wait and see how you feel when you have seen Mary. I will do anything to make you happy."

"Well, I know for sure I don't want to leave Colorado. It's beautiful out here."

He looked around him. "It sure is. Guess I was too blind to see it."

"Its perfect for bringing up children, too."

He waggled his eye brows at her. "Are you trying to tell me you want to start a family?"

"In time, yes, I do. But for now, I am happy with just us."

"Me, too, darling."

CHAPTER 37

"Cathy you look so much better. You are practically glowing," Mary said as she greeted them.

"That's from sweating. Whose idea was it to walk down from the cabin?" she said, teasing her husband. He just smiled, leaving Mary looking from one to another.

"How are you feeling, Cathy?"

"I am really sorry for the scare I gave you, Ben and everyone else. I am fine. I didn't mean to do anything other than have a good night's sleep. I promise."

"I know that." Mary linked arms with her sister. "Why don't you come up to the house and have a bath? We have indoor plumbing so it wont take long. Then you can have dinner with the family. Mrs. Higgins has enough to feed an army, as usual. Abe, you will come too, won't you?"

Abe winked at Cathy as Mary didn't give him a chance to reply but walked off to the house, dragging Cathy along with her. Cathy didn't have the heart to tell her she wanted to be alone in her little house with Abe. They could do that any time. She was limited with the time she had to spend with her sister. Living here on the ranch wouldn't work. Abe was too proud to accept charity and Mary was too generous not to offer it. No, they would go live in Noelle with his ma and sister. She would learn to be a proper housewife and maybe sometime in the near future they could invite Mary and her family to visit.

"Are you happy, Cathy?" Mary asked her as they walked to the bathroom

"More than I ever thought possible, Mary. And to think I owe it all to Archibald. He never did try to hide how much he hated me. Now, I understand. He was always jealous of me and thought I would steal his inheritance."

"Do you mind losing all that money?"

"Not at all."

"I am really happy that horrible man won't benefit from it either."

"Who? Archibald?" Cathy was confused.

"Didn't you hear? He is being investigated for fraud and embezzlement. Seems he has been stealing to fund his lifestyle. He needed your parent's money so badly."

"No wonder he hated me. Yet he would have married me had Papa still been alive."

"You had a lucky escape. I wonder who will inherit the fortune now."

"I couldn't care less. I am so happy, happier than I have ever been. I miss my adoptive parents, they were good to me. But I love being reunited with you and meeting all my new family members. And I have the best husband in the world."

"Now I may just argue that point. There is nobody like Davy Sullivan."

Cathy exchanged a look with her sister and they both giggled like school girls. "Maybe that is one subject we will never discuss. Don't think either of us would win that argument."

EPILOGUE

The party was in full swing, with everyone having the time of their lives. Erin cuddled closer to Mick, who was holding Michelle in his other arm. She spotted Cathy and Abe dancing, their eyes glued to each other. She was sorry they had decided to leave and go back to Noelle but she knew it was the right thing for them to do. Abe was too nice to let his ma fend for herself and Cathy needed some independence. Mary, although her heart was in the right place, was inclined to treat Cathy like a child.

* * *

Erin looked at the happy couple. Wilma beamed, her face lit up like a beacon. She looked so happy and so did the man at her side. Erin hadn't had much chance to interact with Zack, but he seemed like a fine man. He was good for Wilma. More than once, she had heard him telling Wilma to slow down and act her age. It made Wilma mad but he kept doing it. He also had a way of dealing with the twins, who were turning into right little terrors. Between them and Bertram Shaw, the teachers had their hands full.

"Penny for them?"

"I was just thinking how wonderful it is to be back home. With all the people we love and care about."

"It will be even better next month when Mrs. D and the rest of the gang from New York arrive. Can you believe Mr. Prentice is traveling with them? He bought them all first class tickets, too."

"I can believe anything about that man. I wonder whether he will move here permanently?"

"To Clover Springs? I don't know, Erin. He has a lot of business interests in New York."

"Yes, but those he considers family—Robbie and Alicia, for example—live here. I think he might just decide Clover Springs is right for him."

"Who knows, darling. You are usually right, so I am not going to argue."

They danced for a while. Mick nudged Erin, causing her to look up just in time to see Sheriff

Willis lead a blushing Mrs. Grey out onto the dance floor.

"You wouldn't have anything to do with that, my dear husband?"

"Me? Absolutely nothing at all."

Erin smiled at the grin on Mick's face. Mary had accidentally told her about the dancing lessons but she hadn't said a word. She squeezed Mick's hand.

"What?"

"I just wanted to tell you I love you."

"I love you, too, Mrs. Quinn."

* * *

CATHY HELD Abe's hand tighter as Mrs. Shaw and her entourage came toward them. She felt her husband's back stiffen.

"Good evening, ladies. How are we all this evening?"

"Fine, thank you, Mr. O'Malley. Congratulations on your wedding. We were just wondering how your wife was faring. You know, after all her problems."

Cathy stiffened. The woman had some nerve. She was standing right in front of her. Did she think she was deaf?

"My wife is perfect, Mrs. Shaw. I couldn't meet a

better person, and soon we will live in a place where small-minded gossips aren't welcome," Abe said straight-faced. "Darling, shall we dance?"

Cathy had to hold her breath as she tried not to laugh at the look on Mrs. Shaw's face.

Abe pulled her close on the dance floor.

"Abe, people are staring."

"Let them. They are just jealous you have such a handsome husband."

Cathy giggled as he tickled her neck with his nose before he took her into his arms and danced as properly as any other couple on the dance floor. She caught Mary's glance and smiled back at her sister. Mary had done her best to persuade them to stay in Clover Spring, but eventually she had seen Cathy's place was beside her husband. They had promised to visit and to write regularly.

"Happy, Mrs. O'Malley?"

"Yes, darling. So happy."

* * *

AND FINALLY, the next book tells the story of Mrs. Grey who started as a hated character but gradually gained the admiration of a legion of Clover Springs Fans. You can find her story here.

ALSO BY RACHEL WESSON

The Resistance Sisters

Darkness Falls

Light Rises

Hearts at War

When's Mummy Coming

A Mother's Promise

WWII Irish Stand Alone

Stolen from her Mother

Orphans of Hope House

Home for unloved Orphans (Orphans of Hope House 1)

Baby on the Doorstep (Orphans of Hope House 2)

Women and War

Gracie under Fire

Penny's Secret Mission

Molly's Flight

Hearts on the Rails

Orphan Train Escape

Orphan Train Trials

Orphan Train Christmas

Orphan Train Tragedy

Orphan Train Strike

Orphan Train Disaster

Trail of Hearts - Oregon Trail Series

Oregon Bound (book 1)

Oregon Dreams (book 2)

Oregon Destiny (book 3)

Oregon Discovery (book 4)

Oregon Disaster (book 5)

12 Days of Christmas - co -authored series.

The Maid - book 8

Clover Springs Mail Order Brides

Katie (Book 1)

Mary (Book 2)

Sorcha (Book 3)

Emer (Book 4)

Laura (Book 5)

Ellen (Book 6)

Thanksgiving in Clover Springs (book 7)

Christmas in Clover Springs (book8)

Erin (Book 9)

Eleanor (book 10)

Cathy (book 11)

Mrs. Grey

Clover Springs East

New York Bound (book 1)

New York Storm (book 2)

New York Hope (book 3)

ACKNOWLEDGMENTS

These books wouldn't have been possible without the help of so many people. Thanks to Erin Dameron-Hill for my fantastic covers. Erin is a gifted artist who makes my characters come to life.

The ladies from Pioneer Hearts who volunteered to proofread my book. Special thanks go to Marlene Larsen, Cindy Nipper, Janet Lesley, Robin Malek, Meisje Sanders Arcuri and Denise Cervantes who all spotted errors that had slipped through.

Last, but by no means least, huge thanks and love to my husband and my three children.

Come join us at https://www.facebook.com/groups/rachelwessonsreaders

Printed in Great Britain
by Amazon

61598987R00133